Séb blew out a breath. "I'm sorry. There isn't an easy way to put this."

"Then tell me straight," Louisa said.

"Louis Gallet was the heir to the throne of Charlmoux."

"What?" She stared at him, those gorgeous brown eyes wide with shock. "You're telling me my father was a prince?"

"I would say that the man who married your mother and was named on your birth certificate as your father was the prince of Charlmoux."

"Named as my father," she repeated. "That's insinuating that my mother was lying."

"No. I'm casting no aspersions whatsoever on your mother's character. You need to take the emotion out of this and look at the facts." Which was what he'd been trained to do over the last nine years. He'd become very, very good at suppressing his emotions. "This isn't just a family business—it's the throne of a country. We need to prove that you really are Princess Louisa of Charlmoux."

"I'm not a princess, I've never even heard of Charlmoux, and I don't want the throne," she said.

His throne.

Dear Reader,

I started this book thinking about writing a secret baby. But what if my heroine *was* the secret baby? And what if finding out who she really was changed *everything*?

It starts with Louisa having no clue that her late father was a prince—and Sébastien discovering that the secret heiress to the throne of Charlmoux will be displacing him. They start on very opposite sides, but Louisa teaches Sébastien to become less starchy. And when the press finds out the secret, Sébastien teaches Louisa how to be a princess.

But Sébastien wants to marry her for duty, and Louisa only wants to marry for love. Can they both get what they want?

I hope you enjoy Louisa and Sébastien's journey.

With love,

Kate Hardy

Crowning His Secret Princess

Kate Hardy

HARLEQUIN

Romance

Recycling programs
for this product may
not exist in your area.

ISBN-13: 978-1-335-73686-4

Crowning His Secret Princess

Copyright © 2022 by Pamela Brooks

For questions and comments about the quality of this book,
please contact us at CustomerService@Harlequin.com.

Harlequin Enterprises ULC
22 Adelaide St. West, 41st Floor
Toronto, Ontario M5H 4E3, Canada
www.Harlequin.com

Printed in U.S.A.

Kate Hardy has been a bookworm since she was a toddler. When she isn't writing, Kate enjoys reading, theatre, live music, ballet and the gym. She lives with her husband, student children and their spaniel in Norwich, England. You can contact her via her website, katehardy.com.

Books by Kate Hardy

Harlequin Romance

A Crown by Christmas

Soldier Prince's Secret Baby Gift

Summer at Villa Rosa

The Runaway Bride and the Billionaire

Christmas Bride for the Boss
Reunited at the Altar
A Diamond in the Snow
Finding Mr. Right in Florence
One Night to Remember
A Will, a Wish, a Wedding
Surprise Heir for the Princess
Snowbound with the Millionaire
One Week in Venice with the CEO

Visit the Author Profile page
at Harlequin.com for more titles.

For Gerard—one day, we'll get back to the Mediterranean...

Praise for
Kate Hardy

PROLOGUE

'SÉBASTIEN, DO YOU have a few minutes?'

No, he didn't. He was wrestling his way through the paperwork surrounding the latest trade negotiations. But Séb noted the grim look on his PA's face. Pascal wouldn't have interrupted him if it wasn't important. 'Of course, Pascal. Problem?'

'Perhaps. I had a visit from the chief archivist, a couple of hours ago.'

The palace archivists usually made an appointment to see the King or the Queen, not Séb's office. This was odd. He frowned. 'What is it?'

'The team found something in Prince Louis' papers. I promised to bring it to you.'

The papers were from a box that had been shelved temporarily and then forgotten about after the Prince's death, more than a quarter of a century before—until a fortnight ago, when a leaking pipe had caused a minor flood in the archives, and the box had come to light again. Since then, Séb knew that the archivists had been working through the papers, carefully logging them.

Pascal handed Séb a cardboard wallet marked with the name of a high street photographic developer.

Séb opened the wallet and took out the thin sheaf of photographs. The first one was of Prince Louis, the only child of King Henri IV and Queen Marguerite of Charlmoux, who was standing with his arm around a pretty blonde woman Séb didn't recognise; there was confetti around their feet. The second photograph was of the two of them outside the city clerk's office in Manhattan. The third made Séb's eyes widen: the woman was holding a bridal bouquet. Was she a bridesmaid, holding it for the bride? Or maybe a wedding guest, who'd caught the bouquet the bride had just thrown?

The fourth photograph made the situation clear: she and Louis were both posed with their left hands displaying their wedding rings, and they both looked deliriously happy.

'I thought Prince Louis died unmarried,' Séb said quietly. 'These photos would suggest otherwise.'

'Indeed,' Pascal agreed.

'Are there negatives? Or any papers in that box that could shed light on what's actually happening here?'

'According to the chief archivist, no. So I did a little discreet research. I wanted to bring you answers, not questions. Except... Well, you can see for yourself.' Pascal took a piece of paper from the file. 'This is a print from a digital copy which I'll forward to you. A notarised print copy is being sent here by special delivery from New York.'

Séb's spine prickled with unease as he took the document. He studied it carefully. It was the marriage certificate of Louis Gallet—using his family surname, Séb noted, rather than his royal title—to English ballet dancer Catherine Wilson, in New York, dated a month before his death. Louis had given his occupation as 'statesman' rather than 'Prince of Charlmoux'.

'So he did get married.'

'And the marriage is legitimate. I've checked. Using his family name is as valid as if he'd signed it as Prince Louis,' Pascal said.

'Is the marriage legally recognised here in Charlmoux?'

'Yes,' Pascal confirmed. 'I also looked up some newspaper archives online, and there were a few press photographs of Louis and Catherine together that summer. Some of the gossip columns speculated that the Prince might be secretly dating the ballerina.'

'If the paparazzi were following them, then

how did they manage to keep the actual marriage secret?' Séb asked.

Pascal shrugged. 'I assume it was a bit easier to do things quietly in the days before the internet. Before everyone had a camera on their phone and could send pictures across the world in seconds. And it was easier to avoid the paps back then, too.'

'Even so.' Séb frowned. 'Why would the Prince of Charlmoux have married someone at a register office in New York, rather than having a state wedding in the cathedral here? It doesn't add up.' Or, rather, it added up to something that was potentially political dynamite. Had Henri forbidden the wedding and then Louis had eloped and married the woman he loved anyway, without his father's permission? Even though Pascal had confirmed that the marriage was legally recognised here, there could still be a scandal. Plus the King's health was becoming frailer. If he had no idea about the marriage, the shock might be too great for him. 'Does the King know?'

'About the contents of the box, or the marriage?'

'Both.'

'I don't know,' Pascal said, 'but I assured the archivist that you would be delighted with his discretion and would wish that to continue, and that you would prefer him to speak to you about the matter for the time being rather than bother the King.'

'Thank you.' And Séb was grateful, too, that his PA had checked the facts discreetly. 'Did you find anything else?'

'I did some more searching, on a hunch. It was the way Louis was standing that made me wonder.' Pascal indicated the photograph where Louis' hand seemed to hover protectively over Catherine's abdomen, then handed over another document. 'Again, it's a print from a digital copy, and a notarised print copy is on its way from England.'

This time, it was a birth certificate. The birth of Louisa Veronica Gallet to Catherine Gallet, in London; the birth was dated seven months after the marriage. Clearly Catherine had been pregnant at the time of the wedding. This time, Catherine's occupation was shown as 'ballet teacher' rather than 'prima ballerina'; it looked as though she'd stopped performing after Louis' death and had chosen a job that would fit more easily around a baby, which made perfect sense to Séb. She'd named Louis on the birth certificate as the deceased father of her daughter.

Séb sat back and stared at his PA, stunned. 'This changes things.'

Prince Louis had had a child. A daughter who was the legal heir to the throne. The Act of Par-

liament naming Sébastien Moreau as the heir
to the throne of Charlmoux would be null and
void. So when Henri IV abdicated at the end of
the summer, as planned, there might be a completely different person on the throne...

'We don't have proof that Louis was actually
the child's father,' Pascal said.

Séb winced, not liking the implication. The
woman in the photograph looked completely in
love with her new husband, and he looked just
as besotted with her. 'Catherine was married to
him. Legally.' Even if the wedding had taken
place in another country. 'And he's named as
the father on the birth certificate.'

'It's all on paper, Séb. I know it's highly likely
that Louisa Gallet is his child, but she can't be
formally recognised as the daughter of Prince
Louis without a DNA test,' Pascal said. 'We
need the physical genetic proof.'

That felt harsh; but Séb had to acknowledge
that it was a valid point.

If Louisa really was Louis' child, that would
change everything.

Séb had spent nearly a third of his life at the
palace, as a king in training. He wasn't actually
related to the royal family; his parents came from
a long line of farmers. But Séb hadn't wanted to
be a farmer. He'd wanted to change the world—
or, at least, to change Charlmoux. To become a

lawyer and work his way up the justice system so he could make sure a miscarriage of justice like the one that had wrecked his best friend Marcel's life couldn't happen again. The headmaster of his secondary school had spotted that Séb was academically gifted and had persuaded his family to let him go to university to study law instead of joining the family business. Séb had won a scholarship to the top-ranking university in Charlmoux, and he'd worked hard to show that he didn't take either his place or his scholarship for granted. He knew his plans wouldn't bring Marcel's dad back, but at least he could help put in the checks and balances to make sure that what had happened to his best friend's family wouldn't happen to someone else.

In Séb's final year at university, the head of the faculty had suggested that Séb should apply for the role of a special advisor at the palace, rather than taking the usual route of qualifying as a solicitor or barrister. Séb had had to sign the Official Secrets Act before he'd even been able to apply for the role, and then he'd discovered that it wasn't just any old advisory role. The job was to take over from Henri IV, who had no legal heir following the death of his son. To be first in line to the throne. To be a king in training, by a royal decree ratified by an Act of Parliament. Which meant he'd *really* have the power to make a difference to people's lives. To make things fairer. To stop things going wrong. To highlight the importance of mental health and how everyone needed access to proper treatment.

How could he turn down an opportunity like that?

The interview panel had liked the quiet, earnest young man and offered him the job. Séb had discussed it with his girlfriend, Elodie, and his family—as far as he could, around the restrictions of the Official Secrets Act—and accepted. He'd applied himself to the job, earned the trust of the King, and had taken on more and more of the older man's duties as Henri's health had declined.

Though now it looked as if everything he'd worked so hard for might vanish overnight: because it seemed there was someone who had a better claim to the throne than he did.

'I assume, from what you said earlier,' Séb said, 'that you've also done some research regarding Louisa Gallet.'

Pascal inclined his head. 'Firstly, her mother. Catherine. She didn't remarry. She died when Louisa was sixteen.' He handed over the death certificate.

Séb read it and winced. Cancer. Catherine had been only forty-one. How sad. He felt a wave of sympathy for both of them: for the young woman cut off in her prime and for the child who'd been bereaved during her teens. 'Being sixteen is hard enough, let alone losing your only parent.' And it struck a particular chord with him: he remembered the summer when he'd turned sixteen, and learned that his best friend's father had died. Marcel's family had moved to the other side of the country, two years before; all Séb had been able to do in support was write letters, make phone calls, and promise to visit Marcel in the school holidays.

He'd kept his promises, but it hadn't been nearly enough. It hadn't stopped his best friend taking drugs to blot out the misery and shame, then needing months of rehab.

Though this wasn't about what had happened to his best friend. It was about Louisa Gallet and his own future.

'So what do we know about Louisa Gallet?' he asked.

'She took a degree in textile management. She works part-time for her family's bridalwear business, and part-time for a heritage organisation, restoring textiles,' Pascal told him.

So far, so respectable. 'Married? Significant other?'

'It seems not. Though I'm sure you'd prefer to see for yourself.' Pascal passed his phone to Séb, with the screen open on the internet. 'There's a tab for each of her social media sites.'

Séb scrolled through them quickly. They were completely unremarkable. No wild parties, no shots of Louisa looking drunk or out of control, no scandal or gossip. No signs of any boyfriend—or girlfriend. Most of the pictures she posted seemed to be of textiles, or the occasional photograph of herself with her cousins. There were plenty of messages on the bridalwear studio's website from grateful brides and teenagers, thrilled with the dresses Louisa had made them. She'd reposted a few scholarly articles about textile heritage; Regency shoes, dresses and bonnets seemed to be among her favourites, along with Renaissance tapestries.

There weren't many photographs of Louisa herself. The most recent one, on the bridalwear studio's website, showed that she had her mother's fine facial features and Prince Louis' colouring. Her brown eyes were wide, and she wore her dark hair in a messy updo. She looked quite serious; Séb had to stop himself wondering what she'd look like when she laughed, and whether her smile would light up a room. How ridiculous. He needed to concentrate on the task in hand. Her smile had absolutely nothing to do with her suitability as a future monarch.

'So she loves history and she's dedicated to her

work,' Séb remarked. Two things that would probably endear her to the people of Charlmoux—and to her grandparents. 'But surely,' he said, 'King Henri and Queen Marguerite know of her existence?' In which case, why on earth had the King insisted on the Act of Parliament to make Séb his heir?

Pascal spread his hands. 'I've made some very, very discreet enquiries with Emil—' the King's PA '—who has also agreed to refer the matter to you. It's very likely that they don't know. All I know for definite is that Prince Louis died in London and it broke his mother's heart.' He paused. 'There's no record of a Catherine Wilson or a Catherine Gallet being at the funeral or having signed the official book of condolence.'

So Louisa Gallet was a secret.

For now.

But if Pascal had been able to find out all this in the space of a couple of hours, so could the media. Rumours could do a huge amount of damage to the country's stability. Séb needed to find out the truth—and do it quickly.

'I assume you have a contact number for her?'

'Yes.' Pascal handed over the rest of the file. 'I guessed you'd want to talk to her and ask her to do the DNA test.'

'Yes. Thank you, Pascal. You've done an excellent job.' Séb's PA was reliable, discreet and they worked well together. Séb knew that Emil, the King's PA, intended to retire when the King stepped down, and Séb would have no hesitation in promoting Pascal when he took over from Henri.

'Let me know whether you need me to make arrangements for you to go to London, or for her to come here,' Pascal said.

'Thank you. I will.'

Once the door had closed behind his PA, Séb stared at the file in front of him.

The situation left him in a quandary. On paper, it looked as if Louisa Gallet could be Henri IV's rightful heir, meaning that she was the next in line to the throne of Charlmoux. Morally, Séb knew he should step aside for the legitimate heir.

Except he didn't want to.

Becoming king meant that he had a chance to make a real difference—and that was important to him. Growing up, he'd been best friends with Marcel, the youngest son of the family who ran the village shop, which was part of a national chain of small shops. When they were fourteen, the chain had accused Marcel's father of embezzlement, sacked him, and taken him to court. Marcel's father had always protested his innocence, but he'd been sentenced to two years in prison. Marcel's family had moved to the other side of the country to avoid the shame and scandal; Séb's own family had stuck up for them, but he knew there had been a lot of spiteful gossip in the village. The mud had stuck and was impossible to scrub off. Moving away had been their only option.

The week after Marcel's father had been released from prison, he'd died. It had taken Marcel another year to tell Séb that his father's death hadn't been an accident; his father had been depressed and taken an overdose, miserable with the shame of having been in prison—even though he hadn't embezzled a single centime. A year after that, it had come out that there was a major problem with the convenience store chain's new computer system. The discrepancies at the shop had all been due to computer error. Marcel's father's name was finally cleared: but it was too late.

Séb had burned with the injustice and had wanted to do something to stop anyone else's family losing someone they loved very much, their home and their livelihood, all because of someone else's incompetence. It was one of the reasons why he'd wanted to study law, and he'd originally planned to work his way up the justice system until he had the opportunity to make changes to the law, to ensure that miscarriages of justice like this couldn't happen again. The chance to become King meant that he could make even more of a difference, and he wasn't prepared to let that go.

He'd worked hard to prove that he deserved the opportunity he'd been given, and he'd prepared fully for the role. Was it all to be for nothing? And how could Louisa—assuming that Louis really was her biological father—possibly take over from Henri IV, when she'd never had anything to do with Charlmoux and had no experience of life as a royal? If she didn't have the right temperament to rule, there was no way Séb was just handing everything over to her.

Or maybe he didn't have to?

Maybe there was a way for her to be the heir but for him to run the country? As the new queen, she'd need a consort. Who better than the man who'd trained for years for the role of king?

But he was getting ahead of himself. The first thing to sort out was the DNA test. Once the results were back, he'd know exactly what the situation was and he'd work out how he was going to manage it. He'd start by setting up a meeting in London so he could talk to her.

He picked up the phone and dialled the number of Wilson & Granddaughters Bridal and Prom.

CHAPTER ONE

'Oh, Louisa. It's amazing. The perfect dream of a dress.' Jess, the bride-to-be, gazed at herself in the mirror. 'I mean, I know I came here last week with my shoes for the final fitting, so you could check the hem and everything, and it looked amazing then, but with the veil on as well, I look…' She stopped, clearly lost for words.

'My baby.' Her mother brushed away the tear that slid down her face. 'You look like a princess. Your dad's definitely going to cry when he sees you, and Kev's going to be knocked off his feet.'

Job done, Louisa thought, smiling at both of them. This was her very favourite part of the job: where the client tried on her dress after the final tweaks, ready for her wedding or the prom. This particular dress had been fiddly; Louisa had hand-made the lace on the bodice and sewn on the seed pearls, as well as edging the veil with pearls. But, with the happiness shining from Jess's face so brightly that Louisa practically needed sunglasses, all the hard work had definitely been worth it.

'You look gorgeous,' she said. 'Now, if you don't mind me taking a picture for our website first, you can take the dress off again and I'll box it up for you. But I advise you not to take the dress out of the box and hang it up when you get home; the beading's heavy and you'll risk tearing the material,' she warned. 'I know you'll be dying to show it to your dad and your bridesmaids, but you're best off leaving your dress in the box until Saturday morning.'

'But won't it crease if I don't hang it up?' Jess asked.

Louisa shook her head. 'Not the way I pack it,' she said with a smile, and took several snaps of Jess in the dress. 'We won't put these on the website until after your wedding,' she said. 'But I'll send you one now, so that way you've got something to show your dad and your friends before the day.'

'But *not* Kev,' Jess's mum cut in. 'It's bad luck for the groom to see you in your dress before the day.'

'Plus you'd lose the impact,' Louisa said. 'Actually, if I were in your shoes, I'd save it so you hear everyone's gasp echoing round the church when they all see you for the first time.'

Jess nodded. 'I'll do that.'

Once Louisa had boxed the dress, folding it expertly and rolling it in acid-free paper so it wouldn't crease, and sent Jess and her mum on their way, she checked her watch. There were forty-five minutes until her next appointment: though this time it wouldn't be a bride. When he'd phoned her yesterday, Sébastien Moreau had said something about heritage. She was slightly surprised that he hadn't made an appointment to see her at the Heritage Centre where she worked two days a week; but she could never resist the lure of working with old fabric. Even though her schedule meant that she should've been working on the detailing of the next wedding dress on her list, she reasoned that she could always catch up with that this evening. It wasn't as if she had a gaggle of men lining up to take her out somewhere.

She set up the table that she and her cousins used when they had an initial meeting with a client, ready to make notes and sketches that she'd transfer to her computer later. Pencil and paper might look a bit old-school, but she always felt her creativity channelled better with a pencil than with a keyboard. Then she headed into their tiny kitchen area, shook coffee grounds into the cafetière, filled the kettle and set out two mugs.

A quick glance at her watch told her she had

half an hour. It wasn't really enough time to work on any of the three dresses she was working on: the seed pearls and lace she was adding to the one that was due for a final fitting next week, working on the seams of the one she'd cut out to sew next, or spreading the bolt of organza across her cutting table and pinning the pattern on for the dress after that. Her restoration work was all done at the Heritage Centre, so there was nothing she could work on from that side of her job at the bridal workshop. Her cousins—the other members of Wilson & Granddaughters—were both out, Sam at a bridal exhibition and Milly at the wholesaler's: so she couldn't help them with any of their projects, either.

Louisa hated wasting time. She was always happiest when she was busy. Maybe she could add a bit more to the piece she was making for her best friend's birthday: Nina's favourite Shakespeare sonnet, back-stitched in flowing script, within a border of embroidered violets.

She'd completely lost track of time when her doorbell rang. Swiftly, she loosened the hoop from the fabric, slid the needle back into its case, put the whole lot into her project box and slipped it into her work bag before answering the door.

'Mr Moreau?' She smiled at the man on the doorstep. He was younger than she'd expected—

maybe a couple of years older than she was—and he was the epitome of tall, dark and handsome. With short dark hair, soulful dark eyes, a beautiful mouth and a complexion that hinted at a Mediterranean heritage, he'd be perfect as the model for a groom in an upmarket wedding magazine. Whoever he was, his suit was beautifully cut, and the material was expensive; Louisa had to suppress the urge to ask him if he'd mind taking his jacket off so she could take a quick look at the lining and the seams, knowing that it might come across as rude to someone who didn't share her love of textiles. And she also needed to damp down that immediate flare of attraction. A man as gorgeous as Sébastien Moreau definitely wouldn't be unattached. Better to assume he was off limits. 'Do come in,' she said instead. 'May I offer you some coffee?'

'Thank you, Miss Gallet. Black, no sugar, please.'

'Please have a seat.' She indicated the two chairs by her table. 'I'll be back in a moment, and then we can discuss your project.'

The photographs really hadn't done Louisa justice, Séb thought. Wearing plain black trousers, a black strappy top and with her hair piled up on the top of her head, she managed to look both professional and creative at the same time. Her smile answered his earlier question: it really did light up the room, and she exuded a warmth and sweetness he hadn't expected. Then again, he supposed that someone who worked with brides and teenagers needed to be warm and sweet, to be able to deal with nervous clients or difficult parents. Given that Louisa looked so much like her mother, he could quite see how Prince Louis' head had been turned by Catherine Wilson.

He glanced round the small but exceptionally tidy room. There was a chaise-longue covered in teal velvet in one corner, with a small coffee table beside it, clearly for the bride or prom-goer's family; a large cubicle with a curtain where he assumed the client would change; this table, with four chairs, where he assumed she'd show sketches to clients; and a small pedestal desk which had a laptop, a desk lamp and what looked like a photograph frame on top of it. There were no untidy heaps of paperwork or scraps of fabric lying around; although he knew that she worked with her cousins, neither of them were on the premises, so her organisational skills appeared to be excellent.

There were no dresses on display; then again, they were all made to measure, so he wasn't that surprised. There were photographs on the wall: all brides and prom-goers, he noticed. It was a fair assumption that the images were of happy clients.

Unable to resist, he stood up and took a look at the photograph on the desk. It showed five women standing under an arch of roses with their arms round each other. Louisa was in the middle, wearing a prom dress, so she must've been about sixteen: not long before her mother had died, then. Catherine was next to her, still recognisable as the beauty from the New York wedding photo, but looking tired and a little gaunt, with a silk scarf tied round her head. Presumably post-chemo hair loss, he thought. On Louisa's other side was an older woman who looked so much like the others that she had to be Veronica Wilson, Catherine's mother. The other two women had similar features to Louisa but were blonde; Séb assumed they were the cousins who worked with her at Wilson & Granddaughters.

The photograph must've been taken during Catherine's last summer. Séb was glad that she had at least had the time to share Louisa's prom. He shook himself. There wasn't any room for sentiment, here. This was business. The whole aim of this meeting was to persuade Louisa Gallet to do a DNA test under medical supervision, so the results would be legally admissible. And then, if the results came back showing that she was indeed Louis' daughter, he'd decided to persuade her to marry him.

He'd just replaced the photograph on the desk and sat down again when she came back into the room, carrying two mugs. 'I apologise for not offering you a biscuit,' she said. 'We don't tend to have them here because crumbs *really* don't mix well with fabric.' She gave him another of those smiles that made him feel weirdly hot all over, and placed a mug on the table in front of him. 'You mentioned heritage on the phone, Mr Moreau. I'm a bit surprised you called me here rather than at the Heritage Centre.'

Séb knew he'd been vague on the phone, and he'd known perfectly well how she'd interpret his words; but this was something that needed to be done face to face. 'It's not actually about textiles,' he said. 'It's about your heritage.'

Her heritage?

Louisa didn't quite understand.

Then again, Sébastien Moreau's surname was French, as was the very faint trace of his accent. And hadn't the father she'd never had the chance to meet been French?

Now she thought about it, Sébastien Moreau was dressed like a lawyer. An expensive lawyer. He had that air about him: quality tailoring, properly shined shoes, briefcase. It looked as if maybe her father's family had despatched him to deal with her rather than sullying their hands with her themselves.

'I don't think so,' she said. 'My mother's estate was settled a decade ago.' And, oh, how she still missed her mother. 'My grandparents are both alive. I think you might be here under some kind of mistake.'

'There's no mistake,' he said, and confirmed her suspicions by adding, 'It's your father's side of the family.'

'Given that you look like a lawyer,' she said, 'I assume you were properly briefed. So you'll know that my father was killed in a car accident, a couple of weeks after my parents' honeymoon.' She pushed the flare of anger back down. It wasn't this man's fault that her father's family was completely heartless, so she wasn't going to take it out on him. 'There has been no contact between his family and my mother's since before I was born. I don't wish for any sort of contact—' not with the kind of people who had not only refused to acknowledge her mother, they'd whisked her father's body back to France and hadn't helped Catherine with her visa difficulties so she could attend the funeral '—so I'm afraid they've wasted your time.'

'There's a matter of heritage that I need to discuss with you, Miss Gallet.'

Louisa straightened her back, lifted her chin, and looked him straight in the eye. 'Let me make it very clear, Mr Moreau. I'm not interested in anything my father's family have to say. I've managed without them for my entire life. If someone has died and left me something, then please feel free to donate it to an appropriate charity. I don't need it and I definitely don't want it.' Any money they might have left her would feel tainted. Blood money. She absolutely couldn't accept it.

'Nobody has died,' he said.

Apart from both her parents. But Louisa knew it wasn't worth making the comment. 'I'm sorry you've had a wasted journey, but I can't see that we have anything to discuss.' She gave him a speaking look. 'If you'd told me this on the phone yesterday instead of pretending that you wanted to consult me about a heritage textile project, it would have saved us both some time.'

'I understand that you have strong feelings regarding your father's family, Miss Gallet,' he said, 'but it really is important. I need a sample of your DNA. That's why I came here in person. It will take only a few seconds to rub a swab on the inside of your cheek.'

'No,' she said.

For a moment, before he masked it, the shock

was visible on his face. Clearly he wasn't used to people not doing his bidding. 'You're refusing,' he said.

'I'm refusing,' she confirmed. 'If you need something in legal terms, then I suggest you contact my family lawyer. Though it really isn't worth the effort, because the answer will still be no.'

Séb was pretty sure that if he told her the rest of it—that she was potentially the heir to the throne of Charlmoux—her reaction would be the same. She clearly wanted nothing to do with her father's family.

Which kind of solved his problem. If she dismissed her claim to the throne, then it would be back to business as usual and he could take over from Henri at the end of the year, as planned.

But.

If Louisa really was Louis' daughter, her claim to the throne was much more legitimate than his own. He didn't want to pretend she didn't exist and rule Charlmoux under false pretences. He wanted to be a fair, just and honourable ruler, and he wanted to make his country a better place. How could he possibly do that if he started his reign with such a huge lie— especially when a miscarriage of justice had wrecked his best friend's life and taught Séb just how important the truth was? He didn't want to be responsible for another miscarriage of justice.

On the other hand, how could someone who knew nothing of her father's country and hadn't grown up with a royal lifestyle—and whose educational background didn't even begin to touch on the things she'd need to know as a future monarch, the way his had—possibly make a good queen?

But those were all steps he could deal with in the future. He needed to deal with the here and now. She'd told him herself what the barrier was to taking this DNA test. So he'd face it head on.

'Miss Gallet,' he said, 'tell me about your mother.'

She folded her arms—not a good sign, because her body language was all about being closed to communication and shoring up her defences—and looked him in the eye. 'I assume you have a dossier on my family. So why don't you tell me what you know about my mother?'

Séb realised he'd underestimated his opponent. Badly. Cross with himself for not doing his research more thoroughly before meeting her, he said, 'Your mother was a ballet dancer.'

'She was a prima ballerina,' Louisa corrected. 'Do you know what that means, Mr Moreau?'

'That she danced the most important role in the performance.'

'Exactly. She was at the top of her profession. To be a prima ballerina, Mr Moreau, you need more than talent. You need to work hard. You practise. You practise over and over and over. You practise until your feet bleed. And then you practise some more.'

He flinched at the image.

'You learn routines,' she continued. 'Sometimes they're solo, and sometimes they're a *pas de deux* so you have to know exactly what your partner's moves are and where he'll be in relation to you on the stage at any given second. You can't get a single step wrong because it will show. Everything has to be crisp. It isn't randomly tiptoeing across a stage, flapping your arms up and down. Every movement is precise. You need to know the techniques upside down and backwards until you're flawless.'

'Got it,' he said.

'No, I don't think you do,' she said. 'Because on top of flawless technique you need heart and soul. You're telling a story to the audience, but you're telling them without the benefit of words and you need them to feel it and live it with you. They need to see the Sugar Plum Fairy as the Queen, showing her strength and grace. Or Giselle dancing her soul away to save Duke

Albrecht from the Queen of the Wilis, because she loves him more than life—even though personally I think she should've kicked him into touch for being a lying cheat. Or Odette, falling in love with Siegfried. It's the music, the movements, the whole thing. You need to dance well enough to break someone's heart and mend it again. That's why my dad fell in love with my mum. She broke his heart when she danced the dying swan—and then she put him back together again.'

Séb shifted in his seat. Since he'd split up with Elodie, he hadn't dated seriously. He'd fallen in love with the quiet lawyer when they'd been students, and he'd planned to ask her to marry him; but everything had fallen apart within six months of him starting his new role as heir to the throne of Charlmoux. Elodie had wanted to become a family lawyer, but the constant press attention had got in the way of her training and her job. She'd hated all the protocol that came with a royal lifestyle, and she'd hated having so little time with him.

'I love you, Séb, and you're a good man,' she'd said, that last night. 'I know you've got a lot on your plate, and I want to support you. But I hardly ever see you—and, when I do, the press are always there. I can't live in a goldfish bowl like this. You need someone who can cope with this way of life and give you the support you deserve.' She'd kissed him for the last time. 'I'm sorry, but I can't do it.'

Love or duty: that was his choice.

He'd asked her for a day to think it through. And he'd realised that he didn't love her enough to give up his chance to make a difference. He'd picked duty. Eventually there would be a royal bride, chosen on the grounds of political alliances and suitability; love wouldn't come into it. And he'd accepted that.

But even Elodie hadn't made him feel the way Louisa was describing. Not even close. It had never bothered him before; so why, now, was it making him suddenly feel as if something was missing from his life?

'My dad first saw her dance in London, and he came to see every show she performed on a Tuesday night,' Louisa continued.

Tuesday being a quiet day, when the paparazzi were less likely to spot the Prince, Séb thought.

'When the company toured *Swan Lake* worldwide,' she said, 'he followed her. He saw her dance in Paris and Rome and Moscow. When the company went to New York at the end of the tour, he proposed to my mum at the top of the Empire State Building. They got married that same week in Manhattan.'

A marriage, Séb thought, that Louis' family very probably hadn't known about.

'They had a week's honeymoon in New York, then came back to live in his flat in London. They were so happy,' she finished softly.

Séb had seen the wedding snaps, the shared look of love and closeness between Louis and Catherine, and knew that she was telling the truth.

Would the King and Queen have become reconciled to the marriage, had Louis lived?

But there hadn't been enough time for that to happen. 'And then your father was killed in the accident.'

'A month after they married. They were back in London; my mum was doing the dress rehearsal for a new show, and my dad was coming to meet her at the theatre afterwards,' she confirmed. 'Except the police arrived instead, and told her what had happened. My mother was distraught. Obviously she contacted his family to let them know he'd been killed—but then they took over,' she said. 'They flew his body back to France, and there were various admin problems that meant she couldn't get there for the funeral. She asked for their help, but they didn't act in time.'

'Maybe they didn't get the message,' Séb said, his skin suddenly feeling too tight.

'Or maybe they did,' she said quietly, 'but they didn't want her there, so they didn't lift a finger to help her when she really needed them.'

It was beginning to seem as if the King had known about the marriage. Had Henri been furious that his son had married without his permission, blamed Louis' new wife for his son's death, and instructed his team to put the admin problems in the way in the first place? Right at that moment, Séb didn't know the facts, but what Louisa was telling him added up to something potentially heartbreaking. 'People react in ways they otherwise might not, when they're grieving,' he said, thinking of how Marcel had dropped out of sixth form and gone into a spiral of drink and drugs to blot out the pain of loss, after his father's death. It had taken months of rehab before Marcel had dried out; then Séb had persuaded his family to offer Marcel a job to help support him.

'My mum was grieving, too,' Louisa pointed out. 'My dad was the love of her life. She never found anyone who matched up to him. She never even *dated* anyone, after he died. And I should've been able to bury her next to my dad, instead of having to bury her in a different country.'

And now Séb felt guilty on behalf of his country. It looked as if the royal family of Charlmoux hadn't treated Catherine Wilson well at all. 'I'm sorry,' he said.

'So am I,' she said grimly.

But why had Catherine kept Louisa's existence secret from Louis' family? 'She didn't tell them about you,' he said.

'Given the circumstances, are you surprised?' she asked.

He decided to answer her question with one of his own. 'Don't you think Louis would have wanted them to know about you?'

'Maybe his family would've behaved differently towards my mum if he hadn't been killed.' She looked at him, her brown eyes cool. 'Or maybe they wouldn't. I don't actually know exactly where he's buried. I've worked out that his family must be rich, because Mum once told me they buried him in a family chapel behind a locked gate. She couldn't even visit my dad's grave, let alone put flowers on it.'

Séb suppressed the insidious flood of guilt. None of that had been his decision. He couldn't apologise on behalf of the royal family, because he had no idea how the King and Queen felt about what had happened. He was completely in the dark. But he couldn't ignore the pain in Louisa's expression, and he wouldn't rub salt in her wounds by refusing to acknowledge her feelings. 'I'm sorry,' he said again.

'It's not your fault,' she said. 'You don't look that much older than I am, so you must have been a toddler when it all happened.' Her eyes narrowed. 'I'm assuming you work for them rather than being one of them.'

Séb knew his position was unusual. Although he had no blood connection to the royal family, he would be one of them at the end of this year—depending on whether or not the woman sitting opposite him was actually Prince Louis' daughter. But it felt way too complicated to explain.

'I work for them,' he said. Which was true, up to a point: just not the whole truth.

'I'm not going to shoot the messenger,' she said. 'But you can tell them from me that I don't want whatever they intended to leave me.'

Even if it was a kingdom? 'Miss Gallet, I understand that you don't want your legacy, but I'd be failing in my duty if I didn't ask you to take the DNA test. If it turns out you're not your father's daughter—'

Louisa stood up, looking outraged. 'So *that's* what they're saying about my mum, now? She was a dancer on a stage, so that means she was obviously a bit too free with her sexual favours and my father could've been absolutely anyone?' She shook her head in disgust. 'For pity's sake. That sounds like something out of the nineteenth century. I never thought France was such a backward country.'

'It isn't, and nobody's casting aspersions on your mother's character or her fidelity,' he said. 'And, for the record, your father's country isn't France.'

'It isn't?' She stared at him in surprise.

'It's Charlmoux. It's a small country on the coast between France and Italy, and we speak French,' he said.

She frowned. 'Mum always said Dad was French.'

'Not *quite*,' Séb said.

'What's this all about, really?' Louisa asked.

'You did say you weren't going to shoot the messenger,' he reminded her.

'I might have changed my mind about that,' she said, sitting down again but still looking cross.

He blew out a breath. 'I'm sorry. I've made a complete hash of this. There isn't an easy way to put this.'

'Then tell me straight,' she said.

'Louis Gallet was the heir to the throne of Charlmoux.'

'What?' She stared at him, those gorgeous brown eyes wide with shock. 'You're telling me my father was a *prince*?'

'The man who married your mother and was named on your birth certificate as your father—

Louis Gallet—was the Prince of Charlmoux,' he said, wanting to be accurate.

'*Named* as my father,' she repeated. 'That's insinuating that my mother was lying.'

'A biological mother is never in doubt,' he said. 'Whereas a father could be.'

She folded her arms. 'You're saying my mum was a tart.'

'No. Absolutely not. I'd like to state categorically that I'm casting no aspersions whatsoever on your mother's character. You need to take the emotion out of this and look at the facts.' Which was what he'd been trained to do, over the last nine years. He'd become very, very good at suppressing his emotions. 'This isn't just a family business: it's the throne of a country. We need DNA evidence to prove that what's on your birth certificate is the absolute truth and that you really are Princess Louisa of Charlmoux.'

'I'm not a princess, I've never even heard of Charlmoux, and I don't want the throne,' she said.

His throne. Séb was very aware of the tension between what was morally the right thing to do, and what he wanted to do. Of course he should cede the throne to the rightful heir; but would she make a difference to the country, the way he planned to do? He'd spent years training for the role, whereas she was a complete novice.

He'd grown up in Charlmoux and understood its history and its people, whereas she'd grown up in a different country and knew absolutely nothing about Charlmoux. It was obvious who would make the better ruler.

Except he might not be the legitimate heir, any more.

And that made all the difference in the world.

He reminded himself that he had a job to do. 'Actually, you might be a princess. And you can't legally renounce the throne, Miss Gallet, unless you're proven to be the heir.' Even then, she might not be able to renounce the throne. The Act of Parliament that had made him Henri's heir had no provisions for this situation, because nobody had known about Louisa.

'Can't you just pretend I don't exist?' she asked.

It was tempting, but it would lead to a lot more complications. 'No. If I can find you, so can anyone in the press. And certain parts of the media aren't fussy about how they spin a story, as long as it sells.'

Her eyes held a touch of fear. Weirdly, Séb found himself not only feeling guilty about putting that fear in her eyes—even though he'd only told her the truth—but also wanting to protect her. From what he'd seen on the website, Louisa Gallet was a talented dressmaker and clearly had what it took to run a successful business with her cousins and her grandmother; she was perfectly capable of looking after herself. But he still had this weird urge to protect her. He couldn't understand it, because he'd never reacted towards anyone like that before.

'I know it's a lot to think about,' he said. 'Why don't you discuss it with someone you trust—your grandparents, say—then meet me for dinner tonight and we can talk about it further?'

'Dinner,' she said.

'I have a suite.' He named an upmarket Mayfair hotel.

She rolled her eyes. 'Of course you do.'

'That wasn't intended to be boastful,' he said. 'I simply wanted to reassure you that it's a safe place. Discreet. Perhaps we could have dinner in my suite; we'll be able to talk frankly without anyone overhearing our conversation and putting either of us in an awkward position in the media. I'll send a car to pick you up. And your grandparents, if you'd like them to come with you—or a chaperone of your choice.' He took a business card from his briefcase. 'You can reach me on this number. I assume I'll see you for dinner at seven, unless you tell me otherwise. Thank you for your time, Miss Gallet.' He reached a hand out to shake hers.

When she took it, his skin actually tingled. He'd never experienced that before, either.

What was it about Louisa Gallet that affected him like this? And what was he going to do about it, given that they were on opposite sides of a quandary?

'I'll talk it over with my grandparents,' she said. 'I'll confirm our attendance or otherwise by five.'

'Thank you,' he said. 'I'll see myself out.'

CHAPTER TWO

WHEN SÉBASTIEN HAD LEFT, Louisa called her grandmother. 'Nan, I know it's your day at the café—' her grandmother met up with her old backstage friends for afternoon tea every Wednesday '—but I've just had the weirdest meeting and I really need to talk to you about Mum and Dad.'

'Come straight over. I'll text Shanice and tell her I might be late or I might need to give it a miss today,' Veronica said immediately.

'Thank you. I was really hoping you'd say that,' Louisa said gratefully. 'See you in a bit.'

It still felt like some weird kind of parallel universe. How could her father possibly have been the Prince of a country she'd never even heard of? Why didn't she know anything about it? How much had her grandparents kept from her? What other secrets were there?

The bridalwear studio made dresses to measure, rather than keeping a stock of ready-to-wear outfits, so they didn't tend to have walk-in clients. There were no appointments in the book for the rest of the day, so Louisa texted her cousins to let them know something had come up and she'd be out for the afternoon, locked up the studio and headed for her grandparents' home. The second that Veronica opened the door, she enfolded Louisa in a hug, and Louisa could smell something wonderful baking in the oven as she followed her grandmother into the kitchen.

'Tea's brewing,' Veronica said, 'and the cheese scones will be out of the oven in five minutes. Your granddad's at the allotment, but I can call him.'

'I love you, Nan,' Louisa said. 'Don't worry Granddad for now. I'm pretty sure you'll have all the answers.'

The routine of setting the table with plates, knives and two large mugs made her feel more settled. And, once she was sitting across the table from her grandmother, fortified with a mug of tea and a fresh scone, hot from the oven and with butter melting on it, she explained what Sébastien Moreau had told her about her father.

'He said to talk it over with someone I trust and then meet him again to discuss it, but I'm sure he's barking up the wrong tree,' she said. 'My dad wasn't a prince—was he?'

Then she noticed the expression on her grand-mother's face.

'Oh, my God. Are you saying he was telling the truth and my father really *was* a prince?' She stared at Veronica in shock. 'So how come today's the first time I've heard anything about it—*and* from a stranger, too? Why didn't Mum tell me, years ago? Why didn't *you* tell me?'

'It's complicated,' Veronica said. 'Your mum did what she thought was best, and I agreed with her.'

'Nan, I...' Feeling overwhelmed and not knowing what to say, Louisa shook her head and took a gulp of tea.

'Lou, we all love you very much. Your mum loved you to bits and she was the love of your dad's life, just as he was the love of hers. Don't ever doubt that. And I know you're probably angry right now that we kept this from you—'

'*We?* Who else knows?' Louisa interrupted, aghast.

'Just your granddad and me. That's it,' Veronica reassured her. 'The rest of the family only know what we told them. And it's the truth, as far as it goes: your dad's family were posh and they didn't approve of him marrying your mum, which is why your parents got married in New York instead of having a family wedding in London. And there were some, um, difficulties, so your mum couldn't get to his funeral.'

'This is really hard to take in,' Louisa said. 'Was he really killed in a car accident?'

'In London. Yes,' Veronica said. 'Your mum was in bits, especially when his family took his body back to France.'

'Charlmoux,' Louisa corrected dryly. 'When did Mum find out he was a prince?'

'Pretty much right at the start. Your granddad and I didn't know, at least not until after the wedding,' Veronica said. 'It was obvious Louis came from money—otherwise he could never have afforded tickets for the best seats in the house every week, let alone the flights and hotel rooms when he went to see your mum on tour, and he lived in that beautiful flat overlooking the Thames. But when they came back from honeymoon and told us who he really was… Well, once we got over the shock, we could understand why they did it. Your dad just wanted to marry your mum, without all the red tape and the nonsense.' She sighed. 'I wish we'd been at the wedding. I always thought I'd make your mum's wedding dress and your granddad would walk her down the aisle of the church where we got married. But getting married in New York was easier for him. They really loved each other and they wanted to be together, so the register office in New York it was.' She bit her lip. 'I would've given anything for them to grow old together, the way me and your granddad have.'

'Mum always said she wished you and Granddad had been at the wedding, and she'd worn a dress you made—they were her only regrets,' Louisa said, feeling tears prick the back of her eyelids. 'So why didn't she go to my dad's funeral? And I mean *really*, not just what she told me?'

'She tried. There were visa problems.'

'What sort of problems?' Louisa asked.

'I don't know, love. I don't think she ever found out, either. But they took her into a little room and made her wait. Kept her there for hours. Every time she asked what was going on, they said they were waiting to hear. She kept asking if someone would call the King's private secretary or the ambassador, but they kept telling her to wait. In the end, by the time they decided she could leave, it was too late for her to get to the funeral.'

Louisa had a nasty feeling about this. 'Did they arrange that?'

'We don't actually know that for sure,' Veronica said. 'But, I admit, I always thought that was the most likely reason.' She shook her head. 'I could never understand the Queen. I mean, when your uncles fell in love, I couldn't wait to meet the girls they were courting and welcome them to the family.' She shrugged. 'I guess it's different if you're a queen.'

'A few of our clients at the Heritage Centre are minor royals,' Louisa said, 'and they seem normal enough. So I think a queen would probably feel the same way that you did.' She paused. 'If Mum couldn't go to the funeral, how did she find out where my dad was buried?'

'She went to Charlmoux to try to see his family, once she'd got over the morning sickness. I went with her, because I wasn't leaving her to face them on her own. We looked round the cathedral, because she knew Louis had been christened there, and we got talking to one of the guides. He told us the royal family was all buried there, and showed us one of the private chapels; he said Prince Louis had been buried there a couple of months before. We could see his grave through the ironwork of the locked grille, but that was as close as we could get.'

'They wouldn't even unlock the door for his *wife*?' Louisa stared at her grandmother, shocked.

'The royal family didn't accept her as his wife, even though they were legally married. They refused to see her,' Veronica said quietly. 'Cathy tried, but they wouldn't even let her talk to one of the ladies in waiting or what have you.

That's when she decided not to tell them about you. She thought they wouldn't believe her—or, worse, that they'd take her to court and take you away from her and she'd never see you again. Just like the way they made her leave the flat she lived in with Louis, because it belonged to the royal family and not to Louis himself.' Her expression hardened. 'I wrote to the King when your mum died, but I never got an answer. Though I didn't tell him about you, because I knew how your mum felt.'

Her father's family had refused to acknowledge her mother, made it impossible for her to attend his funeral, evicted her from the flat she'd shared with Louis and refused to let her visit his grave. These definitely weren't the sort of people Louisa wanted to be involved with, and she could understand why her mother and grandparents had kept her a secret from her father's family.

But.

They'd kept the secret from Louisa, too. And that was what hurt. Why hadn't they trusted her?

'Mum could've told me when I was old enough to understand,' Louisa said, softly. 'I wish she'd told me herself, before she died. This makes me feel as if I'm a dirty little secret.'

'Of course you're not!' Veronica protested.

'Louis would've adored you, just as he adored your mother. He knew your mum was pregnant and he couldn't wait to be a dad. But, after the way his family treated her, she didn't trust them not to hurt you. She didn't want them to slam a door in your face and refuse to acknowledge you.'

Put that way, Louisa could understand her mother's logic.

'But now they've found out about me, Nan. They want me to do a DNA test, when it's completely obvious whose child I am. I look like my mum, and I have my dad's colouring. All they have to do is look at the wedding photos and they'd know.' She clenched her hands for a moment. 'I'm so *angry* that anyone could think my mum was lying.'

'Maybe that's not quite their thinking,' Veronica said. 'If they're saying you're the heir to the country, I imagine they need to tick all the official boxes—and they also have to be *seen* to tick them.' She paused. 'Have you looked anything up on the internet, Lou?'

'Not yet,' Louisa admitted. 'I wanted to talk to you, first. But I have to admit I'm gutted that I've been lied to all these years. That you knew who I really was and didn't say a word.'

'You're Louisa Veronica Gallet—named after your father and your grandmother—and you're gorgeous from the inside out. That was true this morning, and it's still true now,' Veronica said. 'Love, we kept your mum's secret because she asked us to. We never intended to hurt you. We wanted to keep you safe.'

Louisa bit her lip. 'Sorry, Nan. I know. It just feels…' She paused, trying to find the right word. 'Odd, to think I'm somebody different.'

'You're not different. You're still who you've always been. You're still just as brilliant with a needle, whether it's the bridal and prom stuff or your heritage work. You, my darling,' Veronica said firmly, 'can walk with your head held high.'

'But if Sébastien Moreau is right and I'm actually a princess and heir to the throne of Charlmoux…what happens now?'

'That's something you have to decide, love,' Veronica said.

'My life's *here*,' Louisa said. 'I love my job. I love my life. I don't want to give it all up and go and live in some country I've never even heard of, surrounded by people who really weren't very nice to my mum and will probably be just as vile to me.'

'It might not come to that. Let's start by looking up a few things,' Veronica said. She fetched her tablet from the living room, opened a search engine and looked up at Louisa. 'We'll start with your dad. Louis Gallet.'

She flicked to the image on an encyclopae-
dia site. 'There he is, poor lad. I wish he'd had
enough time to meet you.'

'Me, too.' There was a huge lump in Louisa's
throat.

The written entry that went with the picture
was very brief, telling them that Louis was born
fifty-three years ago in the capital of Charlmoux
to King Henri IV and Queen Marguerite, and
died in London twenty-eight years ago. There
was nothing about him marrying Catherine Wilson, and nothing about them having a daughter together.

'But they were definitely married,' Louisa
said. 'Apart from the photographs, I've got their
marriage certificate. The wedding happened.'

'Of course it happened. All her legal documents were in her married name. Including her
passport and your birth certificate,' Veronica
said.

Louisa clicked on the link to Louis' parents.
'They look really cold,' she said.

'Official portraits often do,' Veronica reminded her.

'But it's who they really are,' Louisa said
quietly. 'Look how they treated Mum. What
makes you think they'll behave any differently
towards me, even though I share their blood?'
She wrinkled her nose. 'They've sent their law-

yer to make me take a DNA test.' She tapped
Sébastien's name into the search engine, wondering just how senior a lawyer he was, and
sucked in a breath as the page came up. 'I don't
believe this, Nan.'

'What?'

'Sébastien Moreau isn't their lawyer at all.
He's the heir to the throne.' She shook her head,
cross that he'd lied to her about something as
simple as that. What else had he lied about—
deliberately or by omission? 'Apparently he was
chosen by the King's advisors and it's all been
sorted through an Act of Parliament.'

Veronica frowned. 'I don't understand. If he's
the heir, why is he insisting that you take a DNA
test to prove that *you're* the heir? Surely it's in
his interests to pretend you don't exist, or to
get you to sign some papers renouncing your
claim?'

'Maybe that's why I have to take the test first,
to prove who I am,' Louisa said. 'He said something about not being able to renounce the throne
unless I could prove I was Louis' daughter.' She
looked at her grandmother. 'He suggested meeting for dinner tonight, to discuss it. I'm certainly not going to his hotel suite, so I think
we'll bring the meeting forward and have it in
a public place.'

'Good idea,' Veronica agreed.

'Can I borrow your scrapbook, Nan?'

'Yes, of course.' Veronica looked slightly worried. 'Though you're not going to lend it to him, are you?'

'Absolutely not. If he wants to take photos of anything on his phone, that's fine, but the original stays here with you. I just want to show him who Mum was. Where I really come from. And…' she lifted her chin '… I want him to apologise for the way they treated her.'

'I'll get the scrapbook,' Veronica said, pushing her chair back.

Meanwhile, Louisa took Sébastien's card from her bag and called the number on it.

He answered within two rings. 'Moreau.'

If he hadn't been the lying snake who represented her father's horrible family, that gorgeous accent would've made her weak at the knees. And that tailoring. And the memory of that beautiful mouth.

But he was on the opposite side to her. And he hadn't been honest with her. No weakening, she reminded herself. Sébastien Moreau might be gorgeous, but no way in hell did she want to get involved with a man like him. 'Louisa Gallet speaking,' she said coolly. 'Change of plan. I'll meet you at three o'clock, in the café at the Drury Lane Ballet Company's theatre.' The one where her mother had danced. Their meeting would be in public, and it would be on her territory rather than his.

'I have a meeting then,' he said. 'Can we make it four?'

'Compromise. Three-thirty,' she said. 'I'll book a table.'

Was it her imagination, or was there a slight trace of amusement in his voice as he agreed to the new time? Heir to the throne or not, by the time she'd finished with him, he'd be grovelling.

'I'll see you then,' she said crisply, and ended the call.

'Was that him?' Veronica asked, returning with the scrapbook under her arm.

'Yes. He's meeting me at the café at Mum's theatre.'

'Your territory? Good plan,' Veronica said with a grin. 'Do you want me to come with you?'

'Bits of me do,' Louisa admitted, 'but I don't want him to think I'm a child who needs someone to bolster her.'

'You're not a child,' Veronica said. 'But this isn't exactly a normal situation. If you change your mind, just say, and I'll be there.'

'Thanks, Nan. But I'll manage. And you look forward to your Wednesday afternoons. I'm not going to make you miss that, just because I'm having a bit of a wobble.' Louisa hugged her. 'Right. Better sort out all my documents. Thank you for the tea and scones.' She held her grandmother a little bit closer. 'And especially thank you for helping me sort things out in my head.'

'That's what I'm here for, love.' Veronica kissed her. 'Good luck. Let me know how everything goes.'

'I'll bring the scrapbook back here on my way home and fill you in,' Louisa promised.

Back at her flat, she booked a table for two at the café, then put the scrapbook in her work bag along with her birth certificate, her parents' wedding certificate and her passport.

This was the kind of business meeting where she needed to dress up. Even though she would rather have worn a summery dress in the June heat, she chose a lightweight navy suit, teamed it with a silky navy vest top and kitten-heeled court shoes, and took out the rope of pearls her father had given her mother on their wedding day. She didn't usually wear make-up during the day, not wanting to risk any smudges of cosmetics accidentally getting on the fabric she was working with, but this was far from a usual day. She took the pins out of her hair, brushed it and put it up in a formal chignon, then did her make-up. Neutral eyes and strong red lipstick, she decided; then added a pair of dark glasses and headed out to Drury Lane.

Séb managed to finish his meeting early enough to be at the café five minutes before he was due to meet Louisa. He was pretty sure that she'd chosen this place because it had a link to her mother, so it was somewhere she knew well; but he'd wanted the advantage of being here first, so he was able to choose the seat where he'd see her walk in.

Though in some respects he knew this behaviour was ridiculous, treating each other almost as if it were civil war. They weren't on opposing sides. She didn't want to be the heir, and he did. They needed to work together to find a mutually agreeable solution that would be best for Charlmoux.

She was three minutes early. In that suit and pearls, she was breathtaking; she reminded him of photos he'd seen of a young Audrey Hepburn, all grace and beauty. And he was shocked to realise that his heart was actually beating faster. He couldn't remember the last time he'd reacted to anyone like that, and it made him antsy. This wasn't appropriate. This meeting was meant to be about his duty. About doing the right thing.

As she reached their table, he stood up. 'Thank you for coming to meet me, Ms Gallet.'

She inclined her head in acknowledgement, rather than reaching out to shake his hand, and slid into the seat opposite him. 'Nice manners, Mr Moreau. Then again, I'd expect nothing less from the heir to the throne of Charlmoux.'

Uh-oh. He hadn't told her that. Of *course* she would've looked him up on the internet. He should've anticipated that and told her up front.

'Not my father's family lawyer,' she added coolly, 'which you led me to believe you were.'

OK, so he'd omitted some details; but he hadn't lied to her outright. She'd been the one to suggest he was a lawyer; he merely hadn't corrected her assumption. 'Actually,' he said, 'I didn't tell you I was their lawyer. I said I worked for them—which, at the moment, I do. And, for the record, my degree was in law.'

'You're splitting hairs,' she said.

He could argue further and win this particular argument on a technicality, but it wasn't worth it. He needed her to feel that they were on the same team. Time for a strategic retreat. 'I apologise for misleading you, Miss Gallet.'

That took some of the fight out of her, to his relief—that, and the arrival of the waitress to take their order.

'I suppose it puts you in a bit of an odd position,' she said, once they'd ordered coffee. 'My existence, once it's officially confirmed, means that you won't be the heir to the throne any more. Why aren't you just trying to bury the story?'

'Because that would be morally wrong,' he said. 'I can't rule Charlmoux starting out with a huge lie. I need to know the truth.'

'That's very noble of you,' she said, sounding as if she didn't think he was noble in the slightest. 'But that still doesn't tell me *why*.'

He couldn't tell her the full details. That wouldn't be fair to Marcel. But maybe if he told her some of it she'd understand. 'Something happened to my best friend's family, when we were fourteen. A miscarriage of justice. It ripped his family apart and the fallout was...' He grimaced. 'I don't want to betray a confidence, but it was pretty bad. Since then, all I've ever wanted was to make our country a place where that sort of thing couldn't happen again.'

She frowned. 'But how could you do that?'

'Because I discovered I was good with words. With law. So I planned to qualify as a lawyer and work my way up the justice system until I was in a position where I could start working with the constitution and put in extra safeguards. It wouldn't fix things for my best friend's family, but at least it might stop it happening to someone else's. And in the meantime, as a lawyer, I could help people who were in trouble.'

She inclined her head in acknowledgement.

'But, if the truth is so important to you, why did you lie to me?'

'I omitted a few details,' he said, 'because I was trying to be diplomatic. This isn't an easy situation for either of us. I wanted to establish some common ground between us before we discussed the issues.' He looked at her. 'This might not be the most discreet place to do that.' Or to tell her that the King's health wasn't great and he was planning to abdicate at the end of the summer. Séb planned to pick his moment to tell her that particular piece of information, because he'd already worked out that Louisa Gallet had a stubborn streak a mile wide. One which she might well have inherited from her grandfather.

'All right. Let's try to talk obliquely,' she said. 'If the DNA test proves the identity of your client's granddaughter, then she can renounce the throne and the heir can carry on?'

'Honest answer? I don't actually know,' he said. 'There isn't a precedent.'

'I don't understand why there wasn't an heir after your client's son died,' she said. 'Surely there's some distant cousin who can inherit?'

Séb shook his head. 'He came from a long line of only children. We'd have to go back so far that any relative would be incredibly distant. The constitution says that if the next in line to the throne isn't within three degrees of kinship, Parliament can appoint an heir.'

'Did the appointed heir know about me when he was appointed?' Louisa asked.

'No. He didn't even know that my client's son was married,' Séb said, 'let alone that a child existed.'

'So how did you find out?' Louisa asked.

'There was a leaking pipe in the archives, a couple of weeks ago. When the archivists moved things from the shelves, they uncovered a box; I presume it had been brought back from London and then somehow forgotten about,' Séb explained. 'They've been working their way through the contents of the box, and they found wedding photographs. My PA checked some details and traced things forward.'

'None of the online encyclopaedias mention the marriage—or the child,' Louisa said.

'Indeed,' Séb said. If Henri knew about the wedding or Louisa's existence, and Séb still wasn't entirely sure whether the King did or not, then he'd done a very good job of keeping it quiet.

The waitress brought their coffee, and he waited until she'd gone before taking an envelope from his briefcase. 'I had copies of the photographs made for you.'

'Thank you. That's kind.' She leafed through them, and he saw the sheen of tears in her eyes.

'I haven't seen these ones before. They're lovely. My parents look so happy.'

Then he noticed something. 'Those pearls you're wearing. Are they the ones in the photograph?'

'Yes. My dad gave them to my mum as a wedding present.' She lifted her chin. 'She left them to me.'

Did she really think he'd demand them back, when they'd clearly been given to her mother with love? Whatever their financial value, their sentimental value to Louisa Gallet was clearly much higher. In Séb's view, Charlmoux could manage perfectly well without them—and he'd argue that with the King and Queen, if he had to. 'I'm glad you're wearing them,' he said. 'It's important to keep memories alive.'

'I brought photographs, too. Not copies, though,' she said. 'You're welcome to photograph anything you want, or let me know and I'll make copies.'

That was a concession he hadn't expected. 'Thank you,' he said.

She moved their coffee cups. 'They're in Nan's scrapbook, and I don't want to risk anything spilling on it,' she said by way of explanation. Then she took the scrapbook from her work bag and placed it on the table in front of him.

Séb leafed through the scrapbook carefully. There were photographs of Catherine Wilson dancing on stage, and newspaper cuttings about her being made the prima ballerina here at the Drury Lane Ballet Company.

So he'd been right about the link. 'This is where your mum danced.'

She nodded. 'She switched to teaching after she had me—a baby and a touring schedule don't go together very well. They persuaded her to come back for a gala performance in aid of the roof repairs here, so I did actually get to see her dance on stage. I must've been about eight, at the time. It was so special—the kind of thing you always remember. Check out the gallery before you go.' She indicated a wall of photographs on the other side of the room. 'Mum's there. More than once. Make sure you find the *Firebird* picture. She looks amazing.'

For a mad moment, he wanted to scoot over to her side of the table, wrap his arms round Louisa Gallet and hug her. But they were near strangers, definitely not on hugging terms; besides, it had been drilled into him that the heir to the throne didn't act on impulse. He was to remain cool, calm and collected at all times.

'I've never actually been to a ballet,' he said.

'Start with *The Nutcracker* or *Swan Lake*,' she advised. 'They're the most accessible, because everyone knows the story and at least some of the music. I would say try to get tickets for a performance here, while you're in London, because *Swan Lake* is on at the moment; but I know they're sold out for the next month and returns are like gold dust.'

'Maybe I'll get tickets, next time I'm in London,' he said.

And he just about stopped himself suggesting that she joined him.

Not wanting to think too closely about why he might want to spend an evening at the ballet with Louisa Gallet, he went back to looking through the scrapbook. There were a couple of candid wedding snaps that he assumed were from the same set as the ones he'd seen already, with Louis and Catherine laughing in the sunlight as confetti floated down around them. Pictures of Louis and Catherine walking in a London park, their arms wrapped round each other. Of Louis standing with Catherine, his expression tender and his hands resting protectively round her abdomen: obviously, Séb thought, Louis had known about the baby.

Then there were pictures of Louisa with her mother as a baby, a toddler, a teen. He could definitely see both the Prince and the ballerina in Louisa's features.

'Your mother was very beautiful,' he said.

'It's not just the way she looked,' Louisa said. 'She was kind and sweet and generous. Her students all adored her. So did their mums. She was one of those people who lit up a room—the sort who made the world a better place just by being in it.'

She didn't have to say the rest. He could see the moment of bleakness in her eyes: she'd loved her mother dearly and really, really missed her.

He looked back at the wedding photos again. It was clear that Catherine and Louis had loved each other very much.

The kind of love his parents shared.

The kind of love his grandparents shared.

The kind of love Séb had almost found with Elodie, but not quite. And he wouldn't get it because, as the heir to the throne of Charlmoux, his marriage would have to be based on what was best for the country.

Now, he was starting to feel the tiniest creeping doubts. Particularly when he thought about the way his skin had tingled when he'd shaken Louisa's hand, that morning. He'd never felt that kind of awareness before.

If it turned out—as he rather suspected it would—that she was the rightful heir, she'd have to marry for the country rather than for herself. Would Henri insist that she married royalty? Or would the King think that Louisa needed a consort with experience in a supporting role, someone who could help her rule?

'May I take a couple of snaps?' Even though she'd said earlier that he could, he didn't want her to think that he was taking her for granted.

'Sure.'

'And one of you, as you are now?'

'All right.' She didn't smile, as if she'd guessed that he planned to show the photo to her grandparents and was wary about it.

He took the snaps he wanted, then closed the album and handed it back to her.

'So how does the DNA test work?' Louisa asked.

'The grandchild takes a swab from the inside of the cheek,' he said, 'and the lab compares the sample cells to those of the grandparents. Obviously it's not quite as conclusive as paternity or maternity testing, but the lab can determine if there are shared genetic markers. The experts told me if there's a low number, then the test subjects are unlikely to be related. If there's a higher number, then it's as good a proof as we're going to get.'

'And you already have the grandparents' tests?'

He wasn't going to mislead her again. 'Not yet. I wanted to talk to you, first,' he said.

'*If* I do it—and I haven't agreed yet,' she reminded him, 'what happens next?'

'If the report says there isn't a match, then I don't need to bother you any further.'

'And if there is a match?'

'Then you need to think about what you want to do and what's best for the country,' he said. 'If you're Henri's granddaughter, that means you're his heir.'

'Which means you won't be the heir any more.'

'Your birth would take precedence over the Act of Parliament that named the current heir.'

'What will you do, if it turns out you're not the heir any more?'

Propose to her, so he could still do the job he'd trained for.

Though he still needed a bit of time to think that through. To make sure that it was a logical decision, one that really was best for the country, and not one that was based on the unexpected tingles that had thrown him off balance earlier. 'I haven't had time to consider that properly,' he said. 'Maybe I'd move to an advisory role.'

'How long have you been the heir?'

Séb frowned. 'I thought you'd already looked me up?'

'Yes, but I want to hear the story from you.'

He'd give her the bare bones, because Marcel's story wasn't his to tell. 'All right. I'm the second of four boys. Everyone expected me to join the family business—my family are farmers—but I did well at school, and the headteacher persuaded my parents to let me stay on for sixth form and go to university. I told you that things were tough for my best friend, so I wanted to be a lawyer and change things.'

'So you were the only person in your family to go to university?'

He nodded. 'My brothers are all involved with the farm.' She didn't need to know that he'd bought the farm with the money he'd earned, and transferred the deeds quietly to his family. 'I was in my last year at university when the head of the faculty suggested that I should apply for an advisory post in the royal household.' He smiled. 'I had to sign the Official Secrets Act first, and then I discovered that the role was to be the heir. I did the aptitude tests and had several interviews. They offered me the job.'

'And it's what you wanted?'

'I didn't accept straight away. I thought about it for a few days,' he said. 'I talked it over with my family—as much as I could, within the agreement I'd signed.' Louisa didn't need to know about Elodie, either. 'I knew it would mean a huge change in my life.'

'What made you decide to accept?'

'I think I could make a good king,' he said. 'I've grown up outside of a life of privilege, so I have a good understanding of what it is to be an ordinary person.' Like her, though he wasn't going to dwell on that. 'I think my experiences will help me be a fair and honest ruler. And I want to make my country a better place.' One without miscarriages of justice.

'Do you actually want to be King?' she asked.

'I've spent nearly a third of my life in training for the role, so yes.' He shrugged. 'It would be a waste, otherwise.'

'Doesn't it feel restrictive, having to do your duty all the time and having no real freedom in what you do?'

That was exactly why Elodie hadn't been able to cope with the lifestyle.

'There's a little bit of a clash between freedom and duty,' he admitted, 'but I came to terms with that a long time ago.' Though it sounded as if Louisa saw things the same way as Elodie and would face the same struggles. He'd need to manage that carefully.

'The way I see it, you want to rule and I don't,' she said. 'And you've already been named the heir. So why don't you just pretend I don't exist?'

'Because it wouldn't be honest. Even though I wasn't completely open with you earlier, and I apologise again for that. Dishonesty doesn't sit well with me,' he said. 'I've seen the damage that lies can do.'

'Mr Moreau—' Séb realised that she hadn't

once used his first name since he'd first met her, keeping a distance between them '—since you say you value honesty, let me be honest with you. My father's family has never shown any interest in me before. My life's here in London. My family. My friends. I love my grandparents, my aunts and uncles, and my cousins. I love my job; I work with two of my cousins and occasionally with my nan. I love my city. You're suggesting that I might have to give all that up for people who are complete strangers to me. For people who, frankly, weren't very nice to my mum, at a really difficult time of her life.'

Put like that, Séb knew what he was asking of her was completely unreasonable. 'I know it's a lot to ask,' he said. 'But, on the other hand, this is merely a DNA test. It needs to be done under medical supervision, to be legally admissible. It makes sense to do it in Charlmoux, and it will give you a chance to get to know your father's side of your family.'

'Given how they treated my mum, I'm not entirely sure that I want to know them,' she said. 'And I definitely don't want to be Queen. I don't want to spend my life in a goldfish bowl, having to be polite and diplomatic to people I barely know, when I'd rather be working with fabric.'

That was definitely how Elodie had felt. But Elodie had been able to walk away. He wasn' sure that Louisa would have that same freedom to choose.

'As I said earlier, I'm not completely sure whether you can renounce the crown or what the procedure would be, but if you *can* renounce it then you'll definitely have to prove beyond doubt who you are, first,' he said.

She was silent for a while. Eventually, she nodded. 'If I do the DNA test, there are conditions.'

'Name them.' Was she going to ask for money and privilege? he wondered.

'I want to visit my dad's grave,' she said. 'I know he's in the private chapel in the cathedral, because they wouldn't even unlock the gate for my mum to visit him—Nan told me this morning. She was there.'

Séb hadn't known about that. And he didn't approve of it, either. When people were grieving, they needed kindness, not to be turned away. 'I'll make sure that happens,' he said. Even if it meant having a fight with palace officials, or the King himself, Séb would support her in this.

'I want to plant a cutting of the lavender from my mum's grave in a private bit of the cathedral garden, so at least they'll have *something* shared near each other.'

That seemed reasonable to him, too.

'And I want his gravestone or memorial slab or whatever there is amended to say "beloved husband of Catherine and father of Louisa".'

She didn't want money or privilege: she wanted her mum to have recognition. Something whose cost would be measured in pride rather than money. Would it be a price that the royal family of Charlmoux would be prepared to pay? Right then, Séb didn't have the answer. If it were left to just him, he'd do it. The best that he could do was try to persuade Henri IV to have some common humanity—though what he'd learned from Louisa today made him wonder whether the King's formality and distant manner covered something darker. If the King had known about the marriage and about Louisa, then perhaps Henri's humanity had been buried with his son.

'And finally,' she said, 'I want a copy of a photograph of my dad when he was younger. Not the formal ones you can find on official websites. I want to choose a private one, which will stay private, and I'm happy to sign a legal agreement to confirm that nobody will see the photograph other than me and my closest family.'

Séb was pretty sure that Louisa Gallet wasn't the type to sell a story and a photograph to the media. And she clearly wasn't fussed about all the trappings of royalty. She could've asked for land, for money, for priceless jewellery and works of art. Instead, she simply wanted her mother acknowledged as part of her father's life, and a personal memento for herself.

What she'd asked for had very little price, but enormous personal value to her. Séb could see that it was a test: if her grandparents weren't prepared to acknowledge her for herself, then she didn't want to get involved with them. He'd need every bit of the negotiating skills he'd learned over the last few years to make this happen.

'All right,' he said, 'I'll talk to your grandparents.'

'Not my "alleged" grandparents?' she asked wryly.

'Legally, "alleged" would be correct,' he agreed. But he was pretty sure that the DNA test would show a biological relationship between Louisa and Henri IV. Regardless of genes, she was definitely a chip off the old block. 'I'll call you when I've spoken to them, and we can discuss where we go next.'

'Thank you, Mr Moreau.' She stood up. 'I need to be somewhere. Excuse me.'

'I'll pay for the coffee,' he said.

'It's already paid for,' she said, completely wrong-footing him. 'I gave them my credit card details when I booked the table.'

Before he could say another word, she turned round and sashayed away.

And Séb felt as if he'd just been run over by a steamroller.

CHAPTER THREE

BACK AT THE HOTEL, Séb checked his watch. Charlmoux was an hour ahead of English time; although it was later than the usual palace office hours, the King and Queen wouldn't be sitting down to dine yet, so he had time to call them.

This was going to be tricky, and he'd need to be extremely diplomatic.

He called Pascal, who promised to arrange an urgent video call with the King and Queen. Ten minutes later, the call came through to Séb's laptop.

'Sébastien? Pascal tells us you're in London. Is this about the trade deal?' Henri asked.

'Not completely, *sire*. I'm also following up on some leads.'

'What sort of leads?' the King demanded.

He sounded irritable; Séb reminded himself that the King was probably feeling unwell, and the older man wasn't being snappy on purpose.

'I'm sorry. I know I should really have this conversation with you in person, *sire*, *madame*, but this is the best I can do right now,' Séb said. 'The archivist found some wedding photographs. Of Louis.'

'But Louis wasn't married,' Marguerite said.

His mother clearly didn't know about the wedding, then; but what about his father? After what Louisa had told him, Séb was pretty sure Henri had known everything. 'I'm sorry to be the one to break it to you both, *madame*,' he said. 'Our research shows that Louis married Catherine Wilson, twenty-eight years ago, in New York. A month before he was killed.'

Marguerite frowned. 'Married? Are you sure?'

'Yes, *madame*.'

'But—but—why didn't we know about this?'

'She was a dancer. A gold-digger. I was working on an annulment,' Henri said tightly.

Marguerite rounded on her husband. 'You *knew*?' In the brief moments before the Queen regained her composure, she sounded shocked and angry. Because her son had married a commoner, or because she hadn't been there to share the joy of the wedding? Was she angry with the King for keeping it from her? Would she have reached out to Catherine?

But her mask was quickly back in place, and Séb could hardly ask her.

Right at that moment, he really didn't like

Henri, either as his boss or as his king. Nothing he'd learned about Catherine Wilson so far had suggested that she was anything other than genuinely in love with Louis. 'The marriage was legal and it's valid in Charlmoux,' Séb said. 'And I need you both to prepare yourselves for something else. Catherine had a daughter.'

The Queen's serenity slipped again and Séb could see longing in her expression, and the slight sheen of tears in her eyes. 'We have a grandchild?'

'Rubbish,' Henri said. 'How do we even know Louis was the father?'

'We need to do a DNA test to prove things either way, *sire*,' Séb said carefully. 'She's agreed to do the test, but there are conditions.'

'Don't tell me. Money. Land. Influence,' Henri sneered.

'None of those, *sire*,' Séb said, holding on to his own temper with difficulty. 'She wants to visit Louis' grave, and she wants a copy of a photograph of him when he was young—a family portrait, not an official one. And she's happy to sign documents agreeing that it will not be reproduced elsewhere.'

The King scoffed. 'And the rest?'

This was the bit Séb knew was going to be sticky. Not the financial things the King was clearly expecting, but something personal. And

Séb was pretty sure the King would refuse flatly. 'She wants her mother acknowledged on his grave.'

'No,' the King said, just as Séb had expected. 'And she's not my heir. You are. There's an Act of Parliament stating that.'

'It's my duty, *sire*, to point out that if Louisa is Louis' daughter, then that takes precedence over the Act,' Séb said. 'She's within the three degrees of kinship.'

'Do you think she's genuine?' Marguerite asked.

'Yes, *madame*, I do.' He flicked into the photo app on his phone, called up the photo he'd taken in the café, and showed it to them on the screen.

Marguerite swallowed hard. 'I can see my son in her.'

'I can't,' the King said, pursing his lips.

The Queen's eyes glittered as if she wanted to shake her husband. Séb wanted to shake him, too. Violence didn't solve anything, but he wanted to snap the King out of his tunnel vision attitude and make him do the right thing by Louisa.

'Her mother died just over a decade ago,' Séb said. 'She has photographs of her mother with Louis, and not just at the wedding. I've snapped them on my phone and I'll send them over to you shortly. And, as I said, she doesn't want anything financial. She just wants her mother recognised.' He paused. 'She says there were difficulties when her mother entered the country which meant that Catherine was unable to attend Louis' funeral.'

'He was *my son*,' Henri said tightly.

The obstinate expression on the King's face told Séb the thing he'd dreaded having confirmed: Henri had known about the marriage and had ensured that the visa difficulties existed, deliberately keeping Catherine away from the funeral.

'He was my son, too,' Marguerite snapped at him.

It was clear to Séb that, if she'd known, things would have been very different. Hopefully the Queen would help him soften the King towards Louisa. It was the best chance he had of an ally.

'Louis was Catherine's legal husband, *sire*,' Séb said quietly. 'I have copies of the documentation.'

'He should've married someone of my choice,' Henri said, 'and then he wouldn't have been anywhere near London and he wouldn't have been killed. It's *her* fault he's dead.'

Séb reminded himself what he'd told Louisa: that grief could make people act in unexpected ways. 'It was an accident, *sire*,' he said, keeping his voice measured, 'which could have happened anywhere, not just London.'

'Her name's Louisa, so she's obviously named after Louis,' Marguerite said. 'Does she want to meet us?' Her eyes were bright with hope.

'She simply wants to visit his grave and to choose a photograph, *madame*,' Séb said gently. 'Should you wish to be there…'

'No,' Henri said, at the same time that Marguerite said, 'Yes.'

Henri's expression tightened. 'I forbid it.'

'I lost my son,' Marguerite said. 'If we've been blessed with a granddaughter, then I want to meet her, Henri. I want to get to know her. We've already lost too many years. We missed her growing up.'

'We don't know that she's really Louis' daughter,' Henri said again. 'She could be an impostor.'

Marguerite shook her head. 'Look at her photograph, Henri. *Really* look. She has Louis' eyes.'

'No,' Henri said. 'Leave this alone. I don't want anything to do with her.' He stalked out of the room and Séb heard a door slam loudly.

'I'm sorry, *madame*,' Séb said. 'I really didn't intend to cause trouble between you and the King.'

'It isn't your fault.' Marguerite sighed. 'Henri never used to be this…' Then she stopped, as if realising how indiscreet she was being. 'I want to meet her, whatever the test says. My husband doesn't have to know.'

'It's not my place to be involved in any disagreement between you and the King,' Séb said. 'But I was planning to bring Louisa to Charlmoux to do the test. Maybe your paths can cross while she's there.'

'I hope so. Tell Emil what you need from us,' she said. 'We can get the tests organised for the King and myself.'

'Will the King do the test?'

'I'll talk him round. At least, I'll try to talk him round. If I can't, we'll have to manage with just me,' Marguerite said. 'I'll sort out some photographs. Perhaps we can look through them together. And I'll make sure the cathedral officials know that Louisa has my permission to visit Louis' grave.' She paused. 'I could escort her myself, if she'd like me to be there.'

Just what Séb had hoped for. And he was glad to know that at least one of Louisa's paternal family would welcome her. 'Thank you, *madame*. I'm so sorry that this has been a shock for you. I had been wondering…' How could he put this without being offensive? 'If you already knew some of the facts,' he finished awkwardly.

'No. Not at all. But clearly my husband did, and chose not to inform me,' she said dryly. 'It's been a shock, yes.' She shook her head. 'Sébastien, I know I can rely on your discretion. Right now, I'm so angry with him. He kept all this from me, out of stupid, stubborn pride. We could've met the girl our son loved, made sure...' Her voice cracked. 'If Louisa really is my granddaughter, then I want to get to know her.' She swallowed hard. 'I miss my son. I miss him terribly.'

In all the years Séb had known Queen Marguerite, she'd never been so open about her feelings. It surprised him to the point where he didn't know what to say—or how to comfort her, over a video call from the country where her son had died.

'Obviously you've met her,' the Queen continued. 'What's she like?'

'Bright. Articulate.' *Beautiful.* He shook himself. The Queen didn't need to know he found Louisa attractive. And he didn't need to let his libido distract him. The situation was already tricky enough. He smiled. 'I think she might be a little stubborn.'

'Like her grandfather, then.' She gave him a watery smile.

'Potentially,' he agreed.

'Do you like her?'

He liked a lot of things about Louisa. Which probably wasn't a good idea. He couldn't mix things up between his head and his heart. He was committed to the best for Charlmoux.

'Sébastien?'

'Yes,' he said finally. 'I like her.'

'Good. I trust your judgement. Leave my husband to me,' Marguerite said.

'Thank you, *madame*.'

'Sébastien,' she said quietly, 'you're a good man. My son would have approved of you.'

'Even though I just picked a fight with his father?' Séb asked wryly.

'I think,' she said, 'Louis would have picked that very same fight.'

Maybe Louis already had, and Séb had simply taken it up again. 'Perhaps, *madame*,' he said.

'Ever the diplomat, Sébastien.' She smiled at him. 'Let me know when you're coming back.'

'I will, *madame*,' he promised.

Once she'd ended the call, he rang Pascal to fill him in regarding the tests and asked him to arrange the King and Queen's DNA test via Emil; then he glanced at his watch. Would Louisa be in a meeting, or on the Tube? She'd been vague in the café, merely saying that she needed to be somewhere. Maybe a text would be the best way to contact her.

Queen Marguerite has agreed to you visiting the grave, and to photographs. Suggest we do the test in Charlmoux; then you can visit the grave and see a bit of the country while we wait for the results. It should take three days. Let me know when's doable for you. Perhaps we can meet tomorrow evening to discuss? Thanks, SM

Louisa was in her grandmother's kitchen, having returned the scrapbook and filled her in on the meeting with Sébastien, when her phone beeped.

Out of habit, she glanced at the screen. 'It's from Sébastien Moreau. The Queen says I can visit Dad's grave and see his baby photographs.'

'That's wonderful,' Veronica said.

Though she noticed that Sébastien had only mentioned the Queen, not the King. Did that mean the King didn't want anything to do with her?

Not that it mattered. The Queen had agreed to two of the things she'd asked for, and of course they'd need to wait for the DNA test results before they could agree on the lavender and the wording on Louis' grave. 'He wants me to do the test in Charlmoux. Apparently it takes three days to get the results.'

'When does he want you to go? I'm sure Vicky will be flexible with you at the Heritage Centre, given the number of times you've worked silly hours to meet a deadline for her, and Sam and Milly can help with your clients at the studio,' Veronica said.

'I'm guessing they'll want the test done sooner rather than later,' Louisa said. 'Before the media gets a chance to find out. Excuse me, I'll just make a couple of calls.'

She contacted her cousins first, sending them a group message to explain she needed to take a confidential trip to do with her dad's family, and asking if they'd be able to help with her clients.
Sam replied instantly.

Course we can. Any time. This trip—do you want one of us to go with you? Or we can ask our dads to go with you if you need backup? Or Nan?

Her cousins or her uncles. They'd have her back. Her whole family would. And not just because she was the baby of the family: they all looked out for each other. Louisa blinked back the sudden tears.

Thanks, but I'll be fine.

Milly chipped in.

You can change your mind any time. We'll be there. And if you need to go on Monday then do it. We've got your back.

She messaged back.

Thanks. Love you lots. xx

Although it was strictly gone office hours, Louisa knew her boss often worked late, so she tried Vicky's number. It felt cheeky to ask for time off at short notice, especially as she'd already arranged to go in early and leave early the next day, but to her relief Vicky was happy to be flexible about the time Louisa needed.

'That's all sorted, then,' she said. 'Sébastien Moreau wants to discuss it tomorrow evening, but...' She wrinkled her nose. 'I'm not missing *Swan Lake* with you just for him, Nan. I've been looking forward to that.'

'You don't have to miss the ballet, love,' Veronica said. 'But you told me earlier that he'd never been to the ballet, so why don't you suggest he goes with you, instead of me? Then he can see for himself. It might help him understand a bit more about Louis and your mum.'

'But it's not fair to make you miss out.'

'I've seen *Swan Lake* plenty of times over the years. And we can always get tickets to go together, later in the run.' Veronica smiled. 'We can still have dinner together beforehand, like we planned. Rico won't mind putting in an extra chair at our table. Remember, your granddad and I knew Louis. We might be able to answer questions.'

'And ask some yourself?' Louisa smiled at her grandmother. 'All right. I'll ask him, Nan.'

She sent Sébastien a quick text.

Checked with my cousins and my boss. Can have time off next week. Does that work for you? LG

A few minutes later, he texted back.

Probably quicker to discuss than send screeds of texts. Are you busy now, or when's a good time to call you? Thanks, SM

She called him. 'I assumed from your message that now works for you?' she checked when he answered.

'Yes. Thank you for calling. Your timescale works for me. For the test, you'll need your birth certificate, one official form of photo ID and two passport-type photographs that the person collecting the sample can endorse as a true likeness of you.'

He was polite, but businesslike and to the point. For a moment, she wondered what he'd be like when he was all rumpled and passionate, so carried away that he forgot about formality. Every nerve-end tingled at the idea; but then she shook herself. This was already complicated enough. She needed to be businesslike, too. 'I've got a couple of spare photos from when I updated my ID card last year for the Heritage Centre,' she said, 'so I can do all that.'

'Excellent. Pierre—my security detail—and I will pick you up from the Heritage Centre on Friday evening, when you finish work. We'll charter a flight to Charlmoux from London City Airport.'

She hadn't quite expected that. Then again, Sébastien was the heir to the kingdom, so of course he'd have access to a private plane rather than catch a scheduled flight. 'All right. Do I need a visa or anything?'

'Just your passport—and that's more for the DNA test. We'll fly you out and back on a chartered flight.'

'Thank you.'

'And perhaps,' he said, 'we could discuss things a bit more over dinner, tomorrow evening. If you're not comfortable coming to my hotel, I'm happy to book somewhere else.'

'Actually,' she said, 'I already have a dinner reservation tomorrow, with my grandparents.' She took a deep breath. 'I have tickets for *Swan Lake*. I was going with Nan but, as you've never been to the ballet, we thought perhaps you'd like to have dinner with us first, and then come with me to the show. And you'll get the chance to ask them anything you want about my parents.'

There was silence on the other end.

'Mr Moreau?'

'Perhaps, as we might have to work together for a while, we could use first names?' he suggested.

'All right... Sébastien.' Weird. Why were her lips suddenly tingling when she said his name?

'Thank you, Louisa.'

Her name sounded very different, the way he said it, with that very slight French accent. And the tingling in her lips increased. Weirder and weirder. She'd never reacted to anyone like this before. They barely knew each other. And yet...

'And I accept your kind offer,' he said. 'Except I will pay for the tickets and for dinner. That's non-negotiable.'

'You can argue that one with Nan,' she said. 'But I don't rate your chances.'

There was a hint of amusement in his voice when he asked, 'Are you trying to tell me your maternal grandmother is scarier than your paternal grandfather?'

'She can hold her own,' Louisa said. 'Oh, she's asking me to check that you like Italian food.'

'I like Italian food very much,' he said.

'Good, because we always go to Rico's before a show. Nan and Granddad have been going there for ever.' She paused. 'Um…would your security guy like to join us?'

'For dinner? He'd usually stand guard near the exit and he'll wait in the foyer during the ballet,' he said.

'He can join us for dinner, at least. We'll sort out a bigger table. I'll text you the address and time.'

'Thank you. What's the dress code?'

'My family's been involved with the stage for years and we always dress up, out of respect for the performers,' she said. 'So it's up to you. A suit is fine. Or if you want to dress down, that's fine, too.' Not that she could imagine Sébastien Moreau wearing jeans. Though, now she'd thought it, a picture slid into her head that made her feel hot all over. Sébastien, in faded jeans and bare feet, walking hand in hand with her along a beach, the sea swishing over their toes…

'Louisa?'

Oh, help. 'Sorry. I missed what you just said.' And she certainly wasn't explaining why. Fantasising about him was just going to complicate a situation that was already like a piece of metallic thread that had tied itself into unmanageable knots. She needed to get a grip.

'I said I'll wait for your text and I'll see you tomorrow, Louisa,' he repeated.

'All right. See you tomorrow.'

Once she'd changed the arrangements at Rico's and told her grandmother what was happening, Louisa headed for home. Although she'd planned to do some work that evening, to catch up with what she hadn't done during the afternoon, her head wasn't in the right place; she didn't want to make a mistake and ruin the dress while she was distracted. Instead, she spent a while researching Charlmoux. It was still hard to get her head round the idea that she could be the next in line to rule a country.

Sébastien had already told her that the country lay between Italy and France, bordering the Mediterranean Sea. When she looked at the articles online, they told her that the lavender fields apparently rivalled those just a few miles away in Provence. There were pictures of wide sandy beaches with turquoise seas that reminded her of that crazy moment when she'd fantasised about Sébastien. She shook herself and scrolled on through photos of gorgeous countryside and ancient castles that made her itch to explore them and look at the textiles inside. Charlmoux looked like the sort of place where she'd love to go for a holiday—but there was a huge difference between going somewhere for a few days' break, and going to live there permanently, just as there was a huge difference between being a project manager and ruling a country.

Although Sébastien had said that the Queen had given her permission to visit Louis' grave and see the family photographs, she remembered now that he'd said nothing about the King. She had no idea whether she'd be met with chilly formality by the Queen, or even open dislike by the King. Would they see her father in her? Or did they blame her mother for her father's death? She'd need to quiz Sébastien much more closely on the subject.

The internet couldn't tell her much more about Sébastien himself. He rarely seemed to date; then again, as the heir to the throne, he'd probably have to be careful that his girlfriends didn't get the wrong idea. Or maybe he really was just a workaholic who focused on his duties rather than on his personal life. She could hardly criticise him there, given that she rarely dated, either. All her relationships had fizzled out after a few dates, because the men never lived up to her expectations. She wasn't prepared to settle for anything less than her mother had had with her father. True love. The sweep-you-off-your-feet and till-death-us-do-part kind.

The next day, Louisa managed to pretend that everything was just fine while she was at the

Heritage Centre; concentrating on her work
meant that she could push all the worries out
of her head. But all the worries came back as
she walked back to her flat from the Tube station. She had no doubt that the DNA test would
prove the truth of her parentage; but what would
happen then? Would the royal family of Charlmoux just let her walk away from a life she
hadn't chosen and didn't want? Or would she
end up hounded by the media, as Sébastien had
hinted, and be forced to change her life completely, living hundreds of miles away from the
people she loved most?

She shivered. There was still a way to go before she had to make that kind of choice. Tonight was all about giving Sébastien a different
perspective. Showing him what Louis had seen
in her mother.

She showered, brushed her hair and left it
down, and changed into a turquoise shift dress,
teaming it with a chunky necklace and mid-heel
shoes. She met her grandparents at the station,
as they'd arranged, and they headed for the little
trattoria just off Drury Lane.

Sébastien was already there, seated at their
table with a man who she assumed was his security detail. He smiled and lifted his hand in acknowledgement, and her heart gave a little skip.

She couldn't possibly follow in her mum's

footsteps and fall for the heir to the throne of
Charlmoux. Her life and Sébastien's were too
far apart, so how could it work between them?
He was handsome and he dressed beautifully,
admittedly: but admiring his looks was as far
as she could go. She needed to think of him as
a model in a bridalwear catalogue. Keep him
at a distance.

And yet her pulse was practically tap-dancing
as she walked over to the table and he stood
up. She'd never felt this fizzy sort of attraction to anyone before and it made her nervous.
'Mr Moreau—Sébastien,' she corrected herself
quickly, 'I'd like to introduce you to my grandmother, Veronica Wilson, and my grandfather,
Jack Wilson. Nan, Granddad, this is Sébastien
Moreau, the heir to the throne of Charlmoux.'

'I'm delighted to meet you,' Sébastien said.
He shook her grandfather's hand and kissed the
back of her grandmother's hand. 'Mr and Mrs
Wilson, Louisa, I'd like to introduce you to my
bodyguard, Pierre,' he said.

'Call us Ronnie and Jack,' Jack said. 'We don't
stand on ceremony.'

Once all the introductions had been made,
they sat down, and somehow Louisa ended up
sitting opposite Sébastien.

'Jack, Louisa tells me your family's been
coming here for ever,' he said.

'Since it first opened,' Jack said, 'when I was building sets at the theatre down the road.'

'The Wardrobe Department used to come here, too,' Veronica added.

'So you both met through the theatre?' Sébastien asked.

Louisa couldn't fault his manners as he chatted with her grandparents about their work and their family, the arrival of the twin boys that had stopped them both touring and made them take jobs where they could share the care of the children, and then Catherine's arrival. Taking a back seat in the conversation meant she had a chance to study Sébastien. He was polite and showed interest without being overbearing; she would've said it was practised diplomacy, but for the fact that his smile genuinely reached his gorgeous dark eyes.

She also noticed just how unfairly long his eyelashes were. And she was pretty sure that his dark hair would curl when wet, if he let it grow a little longer. She could just imagine him, laughing as he ran hand in hand with her in the street through the rain, trying to protect her from the deluge with his jacket as she unlocked the door to her flat...

Oh, help. Where had *that* come from?

She was going to have to be really careful.

Falling for Sébastien Moreau would be a huge mistake.

'Our Cathy loved coming backstage and looking at all the dresses—well, all the girls in the family did,' Veronica said. 'One day, one of the cast was having a fitting. She took Cathy onto the stage and taught her a couple of dance steps. Our Cathy took to it like a duck to water. She ended up joining the cast when they needed some kiddies as extras for the panto. I took her to tap and ballet lessons, and it was obvious right from the start that she had something special.' She blinked back a tear and smiled. 'Lit the stage up when she danced, our girl did.'

'Did you ever think about following your mother onto the stage, Louisa?' Sébastien asked.

Louisa was glad he hadn't caught her woolgathering and fantasising about him—and even more glad that he'd asked a question she could answer easily. She shook her head. 'Obviously Mum taught me the basics of ballet, and I loved the music she played when I was tiny. I loved it when she used to dance for me, too, but I didn't love dancing enough to put in the kind of work you need to do to make a proper career out of it.' She smiled. 'I followed in Nan's footsteps instead. She used to make clothes for my dolls from the scraps from prom and wedding dresses. Just like she did for my cousins,

Milly and Sam. She made our clothes, too. We all fell in love with fabric and we get on well, so we joined Nan in the business.'

'Though our Louisa's always liked the antique stuff. She came with Cathy and me to the Victoria and Albert Museum when she was tiny, to see an exhibition of theatre costumes that included some of the ones I designed. She fell in love with the dresses, the shoes and the fans,' Veronica said. 'And even now, if we go there, she makes a beeline for the costume section and I have to practically prise her away from the displays.'

That tied in with what Séb had seen on Louisa's social media, and he stored that away for future reference. He'd ask Pascal to check whether there were any special textile collections in the National Museum, or even in the palace itself, so he could at least show her something in Charlmoux that she'd enjoy.

'Lou tells me it'll be your first time at the ballet tonight,' Veronica said.

'It is, Ronnie,' Sébastien agreed. 'She says *Swan Lake* is one of the best ones to see, first.'

'That or *The Nutcracker*. You'll recognise a bit of the music,' Veronica said. 'Our Cathy was stunning as Odette and the Sugar Plum Fairy.'

Séb could see the warmth of love and affection in the older woman's smile as she looked at her granddaughter. Louisa clearly came from a really close family. And this reminded him of summer evenings and Sunday lunches with his own family: everyone talking and laughing, plenty of good food, everyone helping with the chores afterwards. For a moment, he felt a pang of homesickness. He hadn't seen enough of his family, recently, and that needed to change.

The Wilsons talked to him about Louis, too: and over the course of dinner he learned more about the Prince than he had in all the years he'd worked at the palace. The Louis they'd known had been sweet and kind and funny, deeply in love with Catherine, and from the sound of it would've make an excellent king because he had the personal touch rather than being super-formal and distant, the way his father was. A prince who'd learned to cook, under his wife's direction, and had thoroughly enjoyed making a roast dinner for his new in-laws. Even though his Yorkshire puddings had been a disaster, they'd all loved it because he'd made the effort. They'd loved *him*, because they'd obviously seen the man and not the Prince.

For a moment, it unsettled him. Since Elodie, Séb had rarely dated, concentrating on his job. He'd forgotten what it felt like for a woman to see him for who he really was. And what kind of woman would he be prepared to let behind the screens he'd learned to put up as part of his job?

Every nerve in his body screamed the answer: the woman who was sitting opposite him. The woman who'd clearly dressed up for tonight, to pay a compliment to the performers, but there wasn't the slightest bit of artifice about her. The woman who'd loosened her hair and it made him think of how it might look spread over his sofa before he kissed her...

His common sense warned him that he needed to back off. Now. This could get way, way too complicated. He couldn't let his heart get involved. This was about doing the best for his country. Doing the right thing. Making a difference. Emotions didn't come into it.

'So do you go to the theatre in Charlmoux?' Louisa asked.

He was glad that his job had taught him to be able to focus on questions, because he didn't want her to guess how much she distracted him. 'Not often,' he admitted.

'Because you don't like it or because you don't have time?' she asked.

'A bit of both,' he said, wanting to be honest.

'That's a shame. I go to the theatre on the first Friday of the month with my best friend,' Louisa said. 'We don't mind what we see—anything from drama to musicals to stand-up.' She grinned. 'Though I can't quite get her into opera.'

He blinked. 'You like opera?'

'Mainly because I love the costumes,' she said. 'I normally go with Nan. Mozart's our favourite. He has a few good tunes.'

He could tell that she was teasing him, and he found himself really liking this side of Louisa Gallet. That fun, carefree grin made him feel as if the sun had just come out.

Again, the solution to all the problems slid into his mind.

He could suggest it, but he had a feeling he'd meet with a flat refusal because she didn't know him. Somehow, over the next few days, he needed to get to know her better. Find out what they had in common. Make friends with her. And *then* he'd suggest it as a sensible option. Louisa Gallet was a sensible woman, so surely she'd see it was the best solution—for Charlmoux, as well as for both of them?

'What do you do at the Heritage Centre?' he asked.

'Restoration—and that could be anything from dresses to upholstery to wall-hangings,' she said. 'At the moment, I'm working on some bed-hangings that were once a canopy of state.'

'Canopy of state?' he asked.

She took a pad and paper out of her bag

and deftly sketched a chair on a dais with curtains above it. 'Like this,' she said. 'Any British ambassador representing the King abroad was given a canopy and a chair of state, among other things. The bed-hangings I'm working on were made from a red and gold silk state canopy from George III's time. The canopy had been cut down to fit the bed, and I'm in charge of the project to clean and repair them.' She smiled. 'When they took the bed apart, you wouldn't *believe* how much dust was on top of the tester—that's the top bit of the bed.'

She glowed when she talked about her work, Séb thought. Clearly she loved what she did. How could it be fair for him to take her away from all this?

Then again, if she agreed to the plan that was rapidly forming in his head, she wouldn't have to leave it all. She could leave the day-to-day State things to him, and continue working with the fabric she loved; and he would get to rule Charlmoux in her name. The title wasn't important to him, but the chance to make Charlmoux a better place was.

The more he thought about it, the more he was convinced that his idea was the perfect solution, because it meant they'd both get what they wanted. He just needed to pick the right time to suggest it and show her that everyone would benefit.

Dinner was fabulous; the menu was on a chalk board, with only a couple of choices per course, because the chef cooked whatever took his fancy at the market in the morning. Bruschetta, gnocchi with sage butter, a *secondi* of salmon fillet wrapped in courgette ribbons and served with side dishes of tiny new potatoes and garlicky spinach, and the sweetest strawberries Séb had ever eaten in his life, served with vanilla ice cream.

'We need to skip coffee,' Louisa said, glancing at her watch, 'or we'll be late.'

'We'll have coffee at the bar in the theatre with you, Pierre,' Veronica said. 'Then you won't have to wait on your own all evening.'

'I'll get the bill,' Jack said.

'It's already sorted,' Séb said. He held Louisa's gaze for a moment when he explained, 'I gave them my credit card details before you arrived.'

Touché, she mouthed.

'Then, next time, dinner is on us,' Veronica said.

'Thank you. That would be very kind,' he said

They walked down the street to the theatre together, and left Jack, Veronica and Pierre in the bar.

'I meant to tell you,' he said to Louisa as they took their seats, 'you look lovely tonight.'

She smiled at him, clearly surprised but pleased by the compliment. 'Thank you.'

'Is your dress a Louisa Gallet original?' he asked.

She nodded. 'I make most of my own clothes.'

'It's a lovely colour,' he said. 'It really suits you.'

'My favourite. I've always loved turquoise,' she said.

'Like the colour of the sea,' he said, surprising himself. He wasn't usually one for flowery language. What was it about Louisa Gallet that made him say and do things outside his comfort zone?

Then the lights dimmed and the curtain came up. Séb had expected to be a little bored, but he found himself spellbound by the music and movement. And if Catherine had been anything like her daughter, no wonder the Prince had seen beyond the graceful movements and beauty and fallen completely in love with her.

Not that Sébastien was starting to fall in love with Louisa Gallet. This was purely a business relationship. If they could be friends as well, that would make things easier; but the heir to the throne, whether that turned out to be Louisa or himself, couldn't put their duty aside for emotion. There was too much at stake.

At the interval, Louisa checked her phone. 'My grandparents have left,' she said, 'but do you want to go and have a drink at the bar with Pierre?'

'Not unless you do.'

'I'm quite happy sitting here, looking through the programme,' she said with a smile.

'I'll just check in with Pierre.' He tapped a quick message into his phone and was satisfied with the reply.

'So what do you think of the show so far?' she asked.

'It never occurred to me to go to a ballet before, but I understand why you like it so much. The dancers are very good.'

'So you feel how trapped the Prince is?'

Yes. Being with Louisa and meeting her family had made him realise how constricted the royal world was. Though it had been his choice. He hadn't been born into it and had it forced onto him, the way Louis had. The Prince had clearly tried to change the conventions, but he hadn't had time to really make enough changes before he'd died.

Just like the Prince in the ballet.

He looked at her. 'The Prince has to get married to someone suitable, not the swan girl.'

'That's a tiny bit close to home,' she said, as if picking up on the thoughts in his head, 'as is the fact that there isn't a happy ending.'

'Just as well I read the plot before I came here tonight,' he said dryly.

'That wasn't a real spoiler.' She rolled her eyes. 'Everyone knows *Swan Lake* is a tragedy.'

Louis and Catherine had been a tragedy, too.

She seemed to realise that they were heading towards very shaky ground, because she said lightly, 'I'm just warning you now, I always cry at the end of the performance.'

'I'll make sure I pass you a handkerchief,' he said.

'Monogrammed and starched?'

Was that what she thought of him? Then again, he'd moved a long way from his childhood on the farm. Even from his time at university. Perhaps he *had* become monogrammed and starched, over the years, to fit in with the protocols that surrounded him.

'Just plain,' he said, feeling suddenly antsy. He was starting to see the world in a different way, when he was with Louisa, and he wasn't sure that he was completely happy with what he saw. Had he wasted nearly a third of his life, trying to fit in to court circles when he was really still a bit of a fish out of water? But he didn't belong back at the farm any more, either. Or at university. If he wasn't at the palace, he had no idea where he belonged.

Louisa flicked through the programme, seemingly unaware of the unexpected turmoil in his head, and pointed out bits that she thought he'd find interesting. But he found himself being distracted—by her. Her hair looked so soft and silky. How would it feel, threaded through his fingers? And her arm was resting against his, because the seats were narrow. He could feel the warmth of her skin through his shirt. It would be oh, so easy to move his hand and twine his fingers with hers…

He'd managed to get the unfamiliar feelings back under control by the time the lights went down again, but he was shocked to find himself so moved by the performance. Just as she'd warned him, Louisa was wiping at her eyes; he passed her his handkerchief. Not starched or monogrammed. Just as he wasn't starched… was he?

No, because the skin on his fingers felt as if it were fizzing when it touched hers.

'That was wonderful,' she said, dabbing at her eyes. 'I'll wash this and give it back to you tomorrow.'

'It's fine. I'll put it in with the rest of my laundry.'

'I insist,' she said.

He decided to pick his battles carefully. 'OK. But I insist on giving you a lift back.'

'I've lived in London my entire life. I feel perfectly safe on the Tube,' she said.

'My mother probably shares a lot of views with your grandmother,' he said. 'They'd both skin me for not seeing you home safely. So no arguments, OK?'

Louisa knew he had a point. 'All right,' she said. 'And thank you.'

Pierre was waiting for them in the foyer, and escorted them to the waiting car. She didn't think anything of the flash she half saw as she got into the car; plenty of people took group photographs on their phone after a show.

Sébastien was quiet in the car, and Pierre didn't seem inclined to talk either. She gave the driver her address; when he pulled up outside, she looked at Sébastien. 'Would you both like to come in for coffee?'

'Thank you, but I have work to do,' Sébastien said.

At this time of night?

Then again, he'd probably had meetings all day. He would hardly have come to London just to see her, and then waited around for a couple of days while she came to a decision. He could've done this whole thing over the phone. 'Well, thank you for the lift home,' she said.

'No problem. We'll collect you tomorrow at five,' he said.

She remembered then what she'd meant to ask him earlier. 'What's the dress code? Do I need a ballgown or anything?'

'Business dress is fine,' he said. 'Though bring something casual, because we'll go incognito when I show you round.'

'All right. I'll see you tomorrow.' She tried out some of the schoolgirl French she'd been trying to remember. *'Bonne nuit, Sébastien et Pierre.'*

Sébastien looked surprised, before blanking his expression and giving a courtly inclination of his head. *'Bonsoir, mademoiselle.'*

Had she used the wrong word? Most of the French she could remember was from her mother's use of ballet terms. She'd grill Sébastien tomorrow to make sure she used the right terms to the King and Queen, if she actually ended up meeting them.

Back in her flat, she put her dress and his handkerchief in the washing machine on a quick cycle so they'd be dry for tomorrow and she could take the dress with her to Charlmoux, then chose the rest of her clothes for her trip carefully and hung them up so she'd be able to pack quickly in the morning. She set her alarm for half an hour earlier than usual, filled with a mixture of trepidation and excitement. Tomorrow, she'd be seeing her father's country for the first time. Visiting his grave and paying respects on behalf of her mother as well as herself. Maybe she'd meet the family who'd had nothing to do with her for a generation.

Was she doing the right thing? Or would it be more sensible to call the whole thing off? The only people she'd know in Charlmoux would be Sébastien and Pierre. Although Sébastien had been perfectly pleasant to her, the fact remained that her existence and the results of the DNA test were likely to mean he'd lose the job he'd spent almost a decade training for.

If she managed to stay on good terms with him, there was a chance he'd help them both out of this mess by sorting out an Act of Parliament: one which meant she could renounce her claim to the throne and he could rule as he'd planned. And then she could come back to London and life would carry on as usual.

But.

There was that weird tingling business. The way she felt more aware of him than she had of any of her previous boyfriends. There was something about Sébastien that drew her: his quietness, the way he kept everything so private. She'd worked out that he was a man of honour. A man who clearly cared about people close to him. A man who'd given up his freedom of choice so he could change his country for the better. But who was he, underneath all those layers? He intrigued her. What made him tick? How could she persuade him to open up to her?

The questions spun round and round in her head, and she still had no answers by the time she finally fell asleep.

CHAPTER FOUR

THE FOLLOWING DAY, Louisa left the Heritage Centre at five; Sébastien had texted her to arrange meeting her in the car park with Pierre. Just as he'd said, the sleek, anonymous grey car was waiting for them and drove them to the airport.

She couldn't help feeling slightly nervous about this. The DNA test was being done for the benefit of his country, not hers, and she had no idea what kind of reception she'd have in Charlmoux. Hostile? Neutral? Welcoming? Did anyone know about her, other than the royal family?

She was about to ask him more when his phone pinged. He glanced at it and grimaced. 'I'm sorry, Louisa. I need to deal with something. I'm afraid it might take a while.'

State business, she assumed. One of the duties of the heir was clearly to be as economical with information as possible.

She fished in her work bag for the box with

the embroidery she'd been working on earlier, and concentrated on that; being busy was much better for her peace of mind than sitting worrying. Just as well she'd brought a distraction with her, she thought, because Sébastien was busy on his laptop until they got to the airport.

'Sorry about that,' he said.

'It's fine,' she fibbed, though adrenalin prickled through her. Was she doing the right thing, going to Charlmoux?

Because it was a private flight, there was none of the queuing Louisa was used to at the airport. And the plane itself was nothing like the ones she'd travelled on before; the seats were wide and plush and comfortable, with a table between them. It was more like a board room than an aeroplane. The whole thing felt unreal.

'It should take us about two hours to get to Charlmoux,' Sébastien told her. 'We'll eat in about half an hour. I thought you might enjoy trying some traditional Charlmoux cuisine; it's very similar to Provençal cooking.'

'Thank you,' she said. 'That sounds good.'

'If you need to charge your phone or laptop, feel free.' He gestured to a bank of sockets.

She plugged in both. 'Sébastien, I know you're really busy and you probably need to catch up with paperwork or what have you, but would you have time to answer a few questions for me, please?'

'Of course,' he said. 'May I offer you a hot drink, or something cold?'

'Coffee would be wonderful, thanks,' she said.

He asked the stewardess for coffee; Pierre opened a newspaper very noisily, signalling that he considered their conversation to be private.

'So what did you want to know?' he asked.

'Obviously I've read up on Charlmoux, but there's a big difference between reading up on something and talking to someone who actually lives there.' She took a deep breath. 'What are the King and Queen really like?'

Séb didn't have a clue where to start answering. 'How do you mean?' he asked carefully.

'When they're off duty, are they anything like my mother's parents?'

'No,' he said. 'They're more formal. Though I suppose that goes with the territory.'

'Do you see much of them, outside state functions?'

'I have a daily briefing meeting with the King.' He could see from her expression that it sounded cold to her. Strange, even. 'If you mean do I socialise with them, it'd be like socialising with your boss.'

'Actually, we have team nights out at the Heritage Centre, and I like my boss very much. I'd enjoy going out to dinner or for a drink with her,' she said. 'But I take your point. Do you actually live at the palace?'

'I have an apartment in the palace. There are guest apartments there, too. You'll be staying in the one nearest to mine.' He gave her a small smile. 'So at least you'll have a familiar face close by.'

'Right.' She was silent for a moment, as if absorbing his replies. 'Apart from the King and Queen, is there anyone else at the palace who knew my father and could tell me anything about him?'

'Some of the senior staff, and some of the retired staff,' he said. 'I can ask the Queen for you if she'd mind you talking to them about him.'

'Oh. It didn't occur to me that protocol might get in the way.' She bit her lip, anxiety clear in her expression. 'Is there anything I need to know about protocol? Anything in particular I need to say or do?'

She'd be a guest of the royal family during her stay; but the King didn't want her there. 'I'd advise just be polite and be yourself.'

'Right.'

She looked slightly forlorn. 'I'll be with you when you see the King and Queen,' he said, 'so

I'll support you as much as I can. Do you speak much French?'

'I learned French at school. Though I'm rusty on everything except ballet terms.' Her smile faded. 'Will the King and Queen expect me to speak French?'

'No. They both speak very good English. But using a little bit of French might help break the ice.'

'What do I call them? *Votre Majesté?*'

'No. You address the King as *sire*—' he slowed his words and exaggerated the pronunciation for her slightly as *seer* '—and the Queen as *madame.*'

'*Madame?* That seems a bit plain.'

He shrugged. 'It is what it is.'

'Should I be addressing you as *sire*?'

He smiled. 'No. I'm not a king.' Yet.

'Prince, then,' she said.

'I'm not a prince, either,' he reminded her. Just plain Monsieur Moreau. But, if it helps, I would have addressed Louis as *Monseigneur.*'

'Is there any other etiquette I need to know?'

'Can you curtsey?' he asked.

She laughed, and how strange that it made his heart feel as if it had done a backflip.

'My mother taught me ballet,' she said. 'Of course I can curtsey.'

'You don't actually have to curtsey when you

meet the King and Queen,' he said, 'but they'd see it as polite. Or you can shake their hand, but wait for them to extend a hand to you, first. Speak only after you're spoken to, and wait for them to sit or eat before you do.'

'Got it,' she said. 'They take the lead in everything.'

'If anyone else asked me how to behave in the presence of the King or Queen,' he said, 'I'd suggest avoiding personal questions.'

'Except the whole reason why I'm going is personal, so it can hardly be avoided,' she said. 'Is it rude to ask the heir to the throne personal questions?'

He smiled. 'You haven't breached any protocol with me. I'm happy to answer anything you ask—as far as I can, that is.'

She inclined her head in acknowledgement. 'Do the King and Queen want to meet me, or am I your guest?'

'You're my guest,' he said. 'But the Queen will see you this evening.'

He wasn't surprised that she picked up immediately on what he hadn't said. 'And the King won't?'

'He's nearly eighty, and he's not in the best of health,' Séb said. He wasn't breaking a confidence; this was all in the public domain.

'Will he use that as an excuse not to see me?' she asked.

'Possibly. Or he might not actually be well enough to see you. Don't take it personally,' he said.

She glanced at her clothes. 'We tend to dress down at the Heritage Centre. If I'd worn a business suit today, everyone would've asked awkward questions. But I do have business clothes in my case. Will I have time to change before I meet the Queen?'

'Yes.'

'Thank you.' She paused. 'What does the heir to the monarchy do?'

He knew what she was really asking. What would she be expected to do, if she was the heir? 'The heir needs to understand the political and the legal system to deputise for the monarch and ratify Acts of Parliament,' he said. 'There's a diplomatic element as well. I'm involved in trade negotiations—that's part of what I've been doing in London, this week. And I'm the patron of several charities.'

'I assume you have advisors to help you?'

'I do, but if the decision stops with me then I make sure I'm very aware of all the ramifications,' he said. 'I guess it'd be like the way you and your cousins are your grandmother's representatives for different parts of the business.'

'She's pretty much retired and trusts us to get on with it. So, apart from meeting clients and designing the dress they want, we go to trade shows, negotiate with wholesalers, handle the social media and we're involved with trade associations,' she explained.

So she already had some of the skills she'd need as the heir. Which was a good thing.

'We've all got different strengths and we try to share things fairly between us in the business,' she finished. 'But I'm guessing you can't delegate anything from your job.'

'To some extent, I can,' he said. 'But mostly you do your duty with a smile and you don't count the hours you spend working. The job is your life, and your life is the job.'

'Do you mind that?'

No, but Elodie had. 'It's fine,' he said.

He answered more of her questions over dinner, about the country and its people.

'What do you do in your free time?' she asked.

'I don't exactly have a lot of free time.' Then he remembered he was trying to sell the job to her, so if she did become Queen she'd make him her consort. That meant selling himself too. 'I've always been a bit of a workaholic.' That sounded bad, too. He was making a mess of this. Usually he was unruffled and sorted things out with the minimum of fuss. What was it about Louisa that made everything feel so upside down?

'What do you do to relax?' she asked.

'I walk in the palace gardens, and I swim,' he said. 'When I've got a problem I need untangling, swimming means I have to concentrate on the strokes and the breaths, so the problem goes into the back of my head and sorts itself out.'

She nodded. 'That's why I do embroidery. I know it's kind of linked to my job, but at the same time it isn't. I'm concentrating on the stitches and the pattern, so I don't have space in my head to worry.'

What made her worry? he wondered, surprised by the sudden surge of protectiveness he felt towards her.

'Where do you swim?' she asked.

'There's a pool and a gym in the palace compound,' he said. 'Though, if I get the chance, I like to swim in the sea.'

'I love the sea,' she said. 'Growing up in London, I didn't really get to the seaside much.'

'Maybe I can take you to the coast while we're waiting for the test results,' he said.

'I'd like that. Though I didn't pack a swimming costume.'

'I can arrange something for you,' he said.

'Thank you.'

That smile was genuine and sweet, and it made him want to throw caution to the winds, scoop her up and kiss her until they were both dizzy.

Which would be a huge, huge mistake.

He needed her to feel safe with him. To get to know him and relax with him. Because this wasn't about attraction; it was about making sure that Charlmoux would be in safe hands, with someone who'd make a difference.

Relax. That was what they'd been talking about. 'What do you do to relax?' he asked.

'I do a dance fitness class every Monday with my best friend, and I go to the theatre,' she said. 'And you probably gathered from Nan that I love museums. Put me in one with textiles, and I'll be happy for hours.'

Little by little, Séb was building up a picture of Louisa Gallet. The more he saw, the more he liked. The more he thought they might be compatible. The more he thought that marriage could be the best solution for both of them— and, more importantly, for Charlmoux.

He just needed to convince her.

Louisa changed into her favourite business suit and tamed her hair into a more formal updo. Wanting something of her mother close, she decided to add the pearls. Sébastien made no comment when she emerged, though his eyes narrowed slightly. Did he think wearing the pearls was a combative move? But asking him might open up a discussion she really didn't want to have. Not when she was already feeling nervous. Besides, he'd already told her to be herself. This was who she was: her mother's daughter.

It didn't take long to get from the airport to the palace. The nearer they got, the more Louisa's nerves jangled. Part of her would've liked to take Sébastien's hand, for comfort; but he was so self-possessed that she didn't think he'd understand why she wanted the support.

The ends of her fingers tingled with adrenalin as Pierre opened the car door for her. But she straightened her back and held her head high as she walked with Sébastien up the steps to the palace. The three-storeyed building was beautiful, the pale stone pierced by tall, narrow windows and topped by a grey slate roof; to her delight, there were turrets at the corners. In other circumstances, she would've loved visiting a place like this. It was bound to contain gorgeous examples of tapestry and needlepoint.

Once they'd walked through the huge front door, she saw a sweeping double staircase with a magnificent balustrade, and portraits that lined the walls. Her ancestors, she presumed, dressed in opulent robes and golden crowns. Yet she didn't feel any connection to them. She didn't belong here.

'What happens now?' she asked Sébastien.

'One of the footmen will take your luggage to your apartment,' he said. 'We have an audience with the Queen.' He indicated the staircase in front of them.

'Before we go—I wait for her to speak to me first, and then I say *bonjour*?'

'*Bonsoir*—it's a greeting as well as a farewell,' he said. 'Though it's fine if you'd prefer to use solely English when you speak with her.'

These were the people who'd been against her parents marrying and who hadn't even let her mother visit her father's grave. She owed them nothing.

On the other hand, the Queen had given Louisa permission to visit the grave. It was the first step in breaking the ice between them. Ice? More like permafrost, she thought. But if the Queen could make the effort, Louisa would try to do the same. '*Bonsoir,*' she said.

Sébastien's smile on hearing his language from her lips bolstered her no end.

'Come with me,' he said, and this time he tucked her hand into his elbow.

Her skin tingled where his fingers touched her briefly, and she tried to damp it down. He was escorting her formally, as a stranger in this palace. Though she thought that this was also his way of trying to reassure her. And it worked, because with him by her side she felt as if she could cope with anything.

Was this how her mother had felt about her father?

She pushed the thought away. Not now. She was about to meet her grandmother for the very first time, and mooning over a gorgeous man she barely knew really wasn't a sensible idea.

He knocked on the door at the top of the stairs. 'This is the Queen's reception room,' he told her. 'It's known formally as the Cream Drawing Room.'

A footman in navy and gold livery came to the door and had a conversation with Sébastien in rapid French that Louisa couldn't follow.

'He's going to tell the Queen that we're here,' Sébastien said. 'Once I've introduced you, I'm going to leave the majority of the conversation to you and the Queen. I'm there to support you, not to take over. If you need my help, just look at me and widen your eyes, and I'll step in.'

'Thank you,' she said. He'd just made her feel much less antsy about the meeting. And she was glad that he wasn't the type who'd take over and ignore her views.

A few moments later, the footman opened the door fully and allowed them in.

Louisa could see instantly how the room had got its name: the walls were all painted cream and gold, with lots of pictures hanging in wide gilded frames. There was a huge mirror over the fireplace, reflecting the light from the tall window opposite and the enormous crystal and gold chandelier in the centre of the room, and a thick Aubusson rug sat on the polished oak floors.

The sofas and chairs were beautifully upholstered in gold and cream; there was a matching folding screen nearby, as well as a tapestry fireguard that made her itch to take a closer look.

But first she needed to meet the woman who sat on one of the sofas, wearing a plain cream dress with a matching edge-to-edge jacket. The Queen's make-up and coiffure were both immaculate, and she could've walked out of a Parisian high society fashion plate. Her back was straight, and she looked at least ten years younger than she really was. Her hands were resting loosely in her lap, as if she was completely at ease—which wasn't surprising, given how many years she must've lived in this place and how used she must be to meeting foreign dignitaries, Louisa thought, let alone ordinary people like her.

Sébastien gave a deep bow, though he said nothing.

Louisa was really glad she'd changed into her navy suit, though even that didn't feel quite formal enough in these surroundings. She remembered what Sébastien had said about curtseying, and sank into a curtsey.

Though, at the same time, this felt utterly wrong. This was her *grandmother*. Her father's mother. The only time she'd curtseyed to her mother's mother was when Veronica had come to watch a ballet class and Louisa had curtseyed to the audience along with the rest of her class. Veronica always greeted her with the warmest, warmest hug. A curtsey felt much too cold.

Louisa was relieved that etiquette demanded that she waited for the Queen to speak first, because right at that moment she didn't have a clue what to say.

'*Madame*, I'd like to present Louisa Gallet,' Sébastien said.

'Louisa.'

There was no emotion whatsoever on the Queen's face. But Louisa thought she saw a tiny, tiny flicker in her eye, as if the Queen were blinking back a tear and putting on a brave face.

Maybe this was what it was like to be a royal: hiding your feelings all the time. Had that been part of Sébastien's training, too? Was that why he was so self-contained and starchy? What had he been like before he'd become the heir? What was his family like?

Though it was none of her business.

'Louisa, this is Her Majesty Queen Marguerite,' he said.

'Bonsoir, madame,' she said.

There was no change in the Queen's expression, but she spoke in rapid French. Louisa could barely pick out one word in ten. She dredged up her schoolgirl vocabulary when the Queen stopped speaking. *'Pardonnez-moi, madame.* I haven't spoken French since I was sixteen. I'm afraid I didn't follow most of what you said.' She'd tried to be polite, but it had backfired. Her only option now was honesty.

'Then we will speak in English,' Marguerite said, in perfect English. 'Please, take a seat.' She gestured to the sofa opposite hers.

Louisa did so, glad that Sébastien sat next to her.

'Did you have a pleasant journey to Charlmoux?'

'Oui, merci,' Louisa said, determined that she was going to wrestle *some* French words into her side of the conversation, to prove that she wasn't completely flummoxed by the situation.

'The King is indisposed, this evening,' Marguerite said.

Just as Sébastien had predicted: and he'd told

her not to take it personally. She glanced at him, and his dark eyes held encouragement.

'I see, *madame*.' How different this was from the way Veronica would've greeted a long-lost grandchild. Maybe the Queen was waiting for the official test results before she switched into grandmother mode; or maybe she'd always be stiff and remote.

The formality made Louisa feel more and more tense, even though she knew Sébastien had done his best beforehand to try to bridge the gap between them.

Maybe it was time to stop ignoring the big issue. Not looking at Sébastien, so she could pretend she had no idea that she was breaking protocol, she said, '*Merci, madame*, for your permission to visit my father's grave.' She was absolutely *not* going to call him Louis, as if he was a stranger. Regardless of the DNA test, she knew the truth. Louis was her father. 'And for allowing me to choose a photograph of my father. I brought some photographs for you, in return.'

Marguerite looked surprised. 'Thank you.' She paused. 'I believe you are to take the DNA test tomorrow morning.'

'*Oui, madame,*' Louisa said. 'But, if I may speak frankly. I think we both know what the results will show.'

'That Louis is your father,' Marguerite said very quietly.

Louisa hadn't expected the Queen to agree with her, and she was shocked into silence.

'I can see my son in you. Your eyes. You look like the photographs of your mother. You smile like her.'

Louisa noted the Queen's careful wording. *You look like the photographs.* 'You never met my mother?'

'No. I had no idea my son was even dating Catherine Wilson, let alone planning to marry her. Or that you existed. But, once I'd learned about your existence, I looked up your mother on the internet. There are videos of her performances.' There was the tiniest, tiniest movement of the Queen's hands. 'Catherine was very talented.'

The praise was genuine rather than polite, and it warmed Louisa. 'Yes, she was.'

'Had I known,' Marguerite said quietly, 'things would have been different.'

Known what? About her mother? About the wedding? About *her*? Louisa's eyes prickled and she blinked the tears away. 'You can't change the past.'

'But you can learn from it,' Marguerite said. 'All these years when I could have known you.' Her voice was filled with regret. 'I miss my son.'

'I'm sorry that I never knew him. My mum told me about him—obviously not that he was a prince, but that he was a good man. She loved him very much.'

'Perhaps we can talk about him tomorrow. I can tell you about Louis as a little boy, show you the family photographs.'

'I'd like that very much,' Louisa said. 'And I will give you copies of the photographs of him in London.'

'I look forward to that,' Marguerite said. 'And I would like to know more about you. More about your mother.' She looked at Louisa. 'Those were my mother's pearls. She gave them to Louis.'

Louisa had worn the pearls to give her courage. Was the Queen going to ask her to return them?

'I'm glad,' Marguerite said, 'that you wear them. Pearls need to be worn often, or they grow dull.'

Was this acceptance? Louisa could barely breathe.

The Queen stood up. 'But you've had a long journey, and I should let you rest.'

It hadn't been that long a journey. In other words, Louisa thought, the Queen needed a rest. Though it must be difficult, in your late seventies, years after your only child's death, suddenly discovering that you had a grandchild. All the regrets and the what-ifs must be swirling about inside the Queen's head. 'Thank you for meeting me,' Louisa said politely, standing up.

What happened now?

She glanced at Sébastien, who mouthed, *Curtsey.*

Except...that wasn't what she wanted.

They'd already broken protocol. Maybe it needed a little bit more breaking. She stepped forward, and put her arms round the Queen, hugging her the way she would've hugged Veronica.

There was the tiniest, tiniest resistance: and then Marguerite wrapped her arms round Louisa.

'*À demain*, Louisa. I will see you tomorrow,' Marguerite said.

It was a dismissal, but not the snooty one Louisa had expected before coming here. It was a promise that tomorrow they'd talk further. Learn to understand each other. '*À demain, madame,*' she said.

Sébastien tucked her hand through the crook of his elbow again—an old-fashioned gesture, but one that she really liked—and guided her to the door. 'I'll show you to your apartment,' he said when they'd left the room, and led her through a maze of corridors.

'Here you are,' he said, stopping outside a door. 'I'm literally just across the corridor.' He indicated the door opposite hers.

An apartment.

Where she'd be a stranger in a strange house—well, palace—and a strange land.

'Let me see you in,' he said gently, 'or you're welcome to come and have a drink in my apartment.'

'I…'

'Tell you what,' he said, 'I'll grab a bottle of wine from my kitchen and come over. Would you prefer red or white?'

'What I'd really like, right now,' she admitted, 'is a cup of tea.'

'In which case, you'll already have supplies in your kitchen. Shall we?'

She swallowed hard and opened the door.

The sitting room was gorgeous; like the Queen's sitting room, the floors were polished oak and there was a thick rug. The Louis XIV chairs and sofa had gilt frames and were upholstered in blue velvet, and there was a table with a chair that she could use as a desk for her laptop or to work on the embroidery she'd brought with her.

The bathroom was sumptuous marble, the bedroom was all floral chintz with a four-poster bed, and the kitchen was compact but well fitted and very modern. As Sébastien had predicted, it was well stocked; there were four different kinds of tea in the cupboard, a range of soft drinks, and a bottle of white wine in the fridge along with milk and a lemon.

'I'll bring the tea through in a moment—if you'd like to join me?'

'Of course,' he said.

Boiling the kettle and preparing a pot of tea for two made her feel slightly more normal, and Louisa was glad that Sébastien hadn't pressed her to talk about what had just happened, because she hadn't quite processed it yet.

'The English answer to everything?' Sébastien asked with a wry smile when Louisa brought the tray containing a teapot, milk jug, sugar basin and two cups and saucers into the sitting room.

'Most of the time, it works,' she said. 'And thank you.'

'For what?'

'For giving me a bit of space, just now—and also for not leaving me completely on my own.'

'You have a lot to think about, so you need space; and I'm the only person you know here, even though we've known each other only for a couple of days, so of course I'm not going to abandon you,' he said gently.

Her smile made him feel as if she'd just turned

the lights on full overhead. She poured the tea. 'Help yourself to milk and sugar,' she said.

'Thank you.' Milk and sugar weren't what he wanted. What he really wanted was…

No.

He needed to remember why she was here.

And that didn't include fantasising about how soft her mouth might feel against his. This weird pull towards her needed to stop. Now. Before it distracted him too much.

'Tomorrow,' he said, 'the plan is to do the DNA test first thing, before breakfast.'

'The lab will work over the weekend?'

'For this, yes. What time shall I call for you?'

'I…' She shook her head, looking slightly helpless. 'What time do you normally have breakfast on a Saturday?'

This time, he smiled. 'Early, so you tell me when would suit you.'

'How long does it take to do the test?'

'With all the admin, maybe a quarter of an hour,' he said. 'You're very welcome to have breakfast with me afterwards. Then we'll join Queen Marguerite to visit the cathedral before it opens to the public.'

He could see the longing in her face. Then again, he knew how much she wanted to visit her father's grave, on her mother's behalf as well as her own. 'Seven-thirty?' she suggested.

'That's fine. Come over when you're ready. You'll need your passport, birth certificate and photographs.'

'They're all in a folder in my work bag.' She sipped her tea. 'You were right when you said the King wouldn't be there this evening.'

'Because he's not well. I also said not to take it personally,' he reminded her.

'What's actually wrong with him?'

It was public knowledge, so Séb knew he wasn't betraying a confidence. 'He has a heart condition.'

'How, when he doesn't have a heart?' she scoffed. 'I can't believe he kept so much from the Queen. That's terrible. Louis was her son. She had a right to know what was going on.'

'Palace diplomacy,' Séb said, even though privately he agreed with her.

'Dishonesty, more like. And you really want to be a king?' She shook her head. 'I certainly don't want to be Queen, not if that's the price. You're welcome to the throne.'

Which would have been music to his ears, but for the conversation he'd had with Pascal earlier that day. He set his cup and saucer back on the tray. 'It's not quite as simple as that.'

'You said you were good with words—with the law.' Her eyes narrowed slightly. 'Can't you pass an Act of Parliament so you can just circumvent me and carry on as before?'

'Technically, I could draft the wording for one.'

'Does that mean you won't actually do it?' she asked. At his nod, she frowned at him. 'I don't understand. Why?'

'Because the bill preceding the Act wouldn't get through Parliament. Louis was very popular. It's one of the reasons why the King left it so long to organise an heir.' He'd planned to get to know Louisa better and give her the opportunity to know him better, before he made the suggestion. Doing it now might be rushing things. On the other hand, it might be a good idea to plant the idea in her head now. If he gave her a little time to think about it, he was sure she'd come to see the sense of it.

'There is a solution,' he said carefully. 'One that would allow me to rule, and you to do whatever you wish.'

'We already know that.' She rolled her eyes. 'You just have to pass an Act of Parliament.'

'Or there's a simpler, easier way,' he said.

'What?'

'You could marry me.'

CHAPTER FIVE

MARRY HIM?

Louisa stared at Sébastien. She couldn't possibly have heard him right. The man in the elegant suit seated opposite her on the royal sofa looked completely at his ease. As if he'd suggested a business arrangement, instead of what she regarded as something incredibly personal.

He hadn't even *asked* her to marry him. He'd just suggested it as a mutually beneficial arrangement. She'd never heard anything so cold-blooded in her entire life.

Unless, of course, this was a parallel universe. Or she was having a peculiar dream: one that felt real, but it couldn't possibly be because his suggestion was so out of left field.

Or he might have said something else entirely, and her subconscious had replaced it with something ridiculous, simply because—if she was honest with herself—she was more attracted to Sébastien Moreau than to anyone else she'd ever met.

'Did you just suggest that I should marry you?' she checked, trying to keep her voice as even and calm as possible.

He didn't look remotely perturbed. She didn't have the faintest clue what was going on in his head. He was completely inscrutable as he told her, 'As the heir to the throne, you'd need to marry for dynastic reasons. You couldn't just choose to marry whoever you like.'

But her father had. Prince Louis had married the woman he'd chosen—the woman he'd loved. Her mother. Was Sébastien trying to tell her that she wouldn't get that choice?

'That's outrageous,' she said.

'It's simply how things are,' Sébastien said. 'If you marry someone who's not used to this kind of life or not suited to it, believe me, you'll both be extremely unhappy.'

That wasn't true. Her parents had been blissfully happy in the short time they'd been together, and her mum hadn't been brought up in a posh family, let alone royal circles. 'No,' she said. 'When—*if*—I marry someone, it'll be because I love him, the way my mum and dad loved each other. The way my grandparents love each other. The way my cousins and my uncles love their partners.'

He spread his hands. 'I'm merely giving you an option to consider, Louisa.'

Louisa couldn't believe he could be so cool and calm and collected about it. This was the first time anyone had proposed to her: and, instead of the hearts and flowers and sparkles she'd always assumed went with a proposal of marriage, he'd offered her cold, hard reasons. He'd made it feel like an everyday business transaction instead of something special.

'No,' she said.

'You don't have to give me an answer now.'

'My answer will be the same tomorrow, and the next day, and the next,' she said. 'The only reason I'll ever get married is for love.'

That slight incline of the head told her how naive he thought she was. Well, tough. Instead of making ridiculous suggestions, maybe he could put that formidable intellect of his to better use and sort out the Act of Parliament that would release her from any obligation and clear his way to acceding the throne.

'As you wish,' he said, his expression completely unreadable. 'I'll give you some space. You know where I am if you need anything.'

After he'd closed the door behind him, Louisa stayed exactly where she was. Right at that moment, she felt like a fish out of water, miles away from anyone who loved her. She slid to the floor and drew her knees up, wrapping her arms round her legs. It had been a huge mistake to come here. She should've insisted on doing the DNA test in London.

On the other hand, tomorrow she would actually be able to visit her father's grave.

'Oh, Mum. I wish you were here,' she whispered. 'I wish I knew what to do.'

Even though Charlmoux time was an hour ahead of London, Louisa knew it was still too late to call her grandparents. She could call Sam and Milly, but she didn't want them to worry about her. She settled for sending them all a brief text, reassuring them that she was fine and making a joke about managing not to be thrown into the dungeons so far. Then she unpacked, showered, and set her alarm for the morning.

Although the bed was sumptuous, with comfortable pillows and the perfect mattress, Louisa couldn't sleep. The situation rolled round and round her head. She still couldn't believe that Sébastien had asked her to marry him, purely so he could rule the country in her stead. It was ridiculous. Impossibly cold. And to think she'd started to like him. To think she'd wondered what it would be like to kiss that beautiful mouth.

Tomorrow, she thought, was going to be awkward in the extreme.

* * *

The next morning, Louisa woke to her alarm. Her eyes were sore and her head was pounding from a night spent tossing and turning. A shower and washing her hair made her feel a bit better, though she could see in the mirror that her poor night's sleep really showed in the shadows under her eyes. Cross with herself, she used the lightest make-up possible and pulled her hair into a severe bun. Presumably this counted as a business meeting, she thought, and put on a dark grey business suit. Dressed, ready to face him and carrying the documentation she needed, she walked across the corridor to Sébastien's apartment at precisely seven-thirty.

Even though it was a Saturday, he was wearing a formal suit, so she knew she'd made the right call. But again she wondered whether he actually owned a pair of jeans and a T-shirt. Looking at him, she simply couldn't imagine him growing up on a farm, with muddy paw-prints from the farm dogs on his jeans or hair from the farm cats smeared across his sweater. He was a smooth, urbane machine. Part of the palace.

She shook herself. 'Good morning.'

'Good morning. Did you sleep well?'

'Very,' she fibbed, not wanting to admit to just how much his proposal had rattled her. 'Is the doctor here?'

'No. We're meeting her in my office,' he said.

This time, he didn't take her arm as he shepherded her through the endless corridors; Louisa wasn't sure whether she felt more relieved or disappointed, and that in turn made her feel even antsier. How could she possibly want closer physical contact with someone who'd asked her to marry him as a business deal?

In his office, Sébastien introduced her to Pascal, his PA, and to the doctor who was conducting the test.

Louisa handed over the photographs and documentation, and the doctor signed the back of photographs to confirm they were a true likeness of the person whose documents she'd seen and whose DNA she was collecting. She also signed a form from the lab, stating that she'd seen the birth certificate and passport of Louisa Gallet.

The swab took seconds and was completely painless.

The doctor smiled at her. 'All done.' She sealed the swab in a container, which she placed in a sample bag and sealed it; in turn, the sample bag was placed in an envelope with the form. She sealed the envelope and signed along the join where the flap of the envelope met the back. Sébastien and Louisa added their signatures next to hers.

'The lab will be in touch with the results,' she said with a smile, and left.

'Is there anything you need, Mademoiselle Gallet?' Pascal asked, his tone kind.

'Thank you, but I'm fine,' she said.

'I've arranged that access you asked for, Séb,' Pascal said.

It was the first time Louisa had ever heard Sébastien called anything other than his full first name or the more formal 'Mr Moreau'. Was that what his family and friends called him? she wondered. Was he different with them—more relaxed and carefree, a Séb rather than a Sébastien?

'Thanks, Pascal. Can you text me the details, please?' Sébastien asked. 'Louisa and I are with the Queen this morning.'

'Ah. Visiting the cathedral.' Pascal looked slightly awkward. 'I'm sorry that the circumstances of your visit are bittersweet, Mademoiselle Gallet. But I hope you enjoy your stay in our country as much as you can.'

'Thank you, *monsieur*,' she said.

She walked back to the apartment with Sébastien.

'I promised you breakfast,' he said. 'Just to reassure you, there are no strings.'

'Good, because my answer on *that* subject is still no,' she said, glad that he'd been the one to refer obliquely to his proposal.

His apartment seemed similar to hers, though she noticed that his sitting room had bookcases as well as comfortable sofas; she found herself wondering what he read. His kitchen was much larger, and there were what looked like children's drawings attached with magnets to the outside of his fridge. Obviously she couldn't be rude enough to go and inspect them, but it was a fair guess that they'd been drawn by younger family members. It was heartening to see that he was clearly as close to his family as she was to hers.

For just a moment, she could imagine him hefting a laughing toddler onto his shoulders, or sitting on the floor to play a game or read a story to a bunch of children who idolised him and hung on every word; it made her feel all gooey inside. Which, given his proposal, was dangerous. Marriage, for him, wasn't about love and family. It was about duty. That wasn't anywhere near enough for her.

'I thought we'd eat here,' he said, indicating the small table by the window that was already set for two. 'I usually eat breakfast here because it has an excellent view of the palace gardens, and it catches the sun in the morning. Have a seat and I'll make breakfast.'

'Don't you have someone to make breakfast for you?' she asked.

'For coffee and toast? Hardly,' he said. 'Anyway, I've always made my own breakfast. It grounds me for the day.'

Sébastien hadn't forgotten that he came from an ordinary background, then, and didn't expect to be waited on hand and foot. She liked that.

'But I can arrange for the palace kitchens to bring you an English breakfast, should you prefer,' he added. 'And I can make tea if you'd prefer that to coffee.'

'Coffee and toast is fine by me,' she said. Then her manners kicked in. 'Can I do anything to help?'

'No.' He gave her a brief, unexpected smile that made her heart do a backflip. 'It won't take me a second.'

He put bread in the toaster, placed butter and a dish of apricot jam on the table while the coffee brewed, then brought over the coffee, a plate of toast and a jug of hot milk. 'Help yourself. There's plenty more.'

It felt oddly intimate to be having breakfast with him in his kitchen. She couldn't even remember the last time she'd had breakfast on her own with a man who wasn't related to her. And again she thought of his suggestion: *'You could marry me.'*

No. Of course not. It was ridiculous.

And it was even more ridiculous that she suddenly felt shy with him.

* * *

Although Séb had planned not to mention his proposal, giving Louisa the space to think about it and mull it over in her own way, he could see that she looked awkward and miserable. He really couldn't stand by and let her suffer.

'Are you worried about this morning?' he asked, wondering if she'd be defensive and hide the truth.

'No. I think we broke the ice last night, and the Queen and I will come to some kind of an understanding,' she said.

'Are you worried about meeting the King?'

'Yes and no,' she said. 'I'm guessing that his health will be an excuse for him not to see me until the DNA results are back.'

'That's possible,' Séb admitted, 'but, as I said last night, he does have a problem with his heart. He's planning to step down at the end of the summer.'

Her gorgeous brown eyes widened. 'Is that why the DNA test had to be done as soon as possible?'

'Decisions need to be made,' he said. 'Once we know all the facts.'

'You mean, we need the test results,' she said. 'Just to be clear, I have no intention of ruling the country, and I have no intention of marrying you.'

'Is that what kept you awake, last night?' he asked.

She looked away. 'No.'

He knew she wasn't quite telling the truth. It made him feel guilty; yet, at the same time, it was a good sign. She'd been thinking about it. Thinking about him. Just as he'd been thinking about her. But now wasn't the time to push her about it. He needed her to feel comfortable with him; then maybe she'd be more inclined to look at his proposal more realistically instead of giving a knee-jerk refusal. 'It's only one of the options—one of the easier ones, I think, but you have choices.'

'Do I?'

She looked trapped, and it made him feel guilty. He wanted her to feel more at ease. 'Yes. We'll make time to discuss them. But for now let's concentrate on this morning.'

'What's the dress code for today?' she asked.

'What you're wearing now is fine for this morning with the Queen,' he said. 'But, as I said back in London, we need to be incognito while I'm showing you round. I'd suggest changing into something more casual, so you look like a tourist.'

'I *am* a tourist,' she pointed out. 'What are you planning for this afternoon?'

'Something I hope you'll like,' he said. 'Pascal's been talking to a couple of the curators at the National Museum. They've arranged to let you see some things that aren't usually on show.'

She looked surprised, then pleased.

'It's not all bad in Charlmoux, you know,' he said.

She wrinkled her nose, and Séb was shocked to realised how cute he found it. How cute he found *her*. He reminded himself that he needed to concentrate on what was right for Charlmoux and not let himself get distracted.

'I looked up Charlmoux on the internet,' she said. 'I thought it was the kind of country I'd love to visit on holiday—to see the chateaux, walk on the beaches and visit all the museums in the capital.'

'You can at least see some of the museums and the palace while you're here,' he said, 'though I can't promise we'll have time to visit the beach or the lavender fields.'

'What sort of farm does your family have?' she asked, surprising him by switching to something personal.

'Mixed,' he said. 'My brother André deals with the dairy side—we produce organic cheese—Jacques handles the wheat and barley, and Luc works with my best friend in the vineyard.'

'Do you ever feel left out?' she asked.

It was a question nobody ever asked him; and, in a way, he did feel left out. Though it had been his free choice to take the palace opportunity, so he had no grounds to complain about anything. 'We have regular video calls,' he said. 'They send me photos so I can see my nieces and nephews growing up, and I have a supply of drawings for the front of my fridge.'

'But you don't see them as often as you'd like to?'

No, but he wasn't going to admit it. 'Probably not as much as you see your family,' he said. He didn't want to think about his family and how much he'd neglected them for his job. He wanted to concentrate on sorting out the accession to the throne. 'More coffee?'

After breakfast, they met the Queen and her security detail and headed for the cathedral. The building was magnificent, with soaring architecture and beautiful stained glass. The family chapel was behind a locked grille, just as Veronica had described; but the gate was opened for her.

'We'll leave you alone for a while,' Marguerite said.

Louisa looked at the dark grey marble slab with its gold lettering. There was plenty of space to add the words she wanted. She'd brought a white silk rose with her, like the ones in her mother's wedding bouquet, and placed it on a corner of the slab. 'Hey, Dad. So I finally get to visit you,' she said. 'I'm glad I've met your mother. We've started to break the ice. Your father might be another matter, but I'll make the effort—if he'll let me.' She took a deep breath. 'I don't know if you were trying to escape the palace and join a normal family, or if you wanted to bring Mum back here to be your queen. She never talked about it to me and it's too late to ask her, now.' She paused. 'I'm really not sure I'm cut out to be a queen. I love what I do and I love working with my family. Even if you'd lived and you'd brought me up here, I think I would still have loved fabric and wanted to work with Nan.' And she might have had younger brothers or sisters who were much more suited to the role of ruler; she wouldn't have minded stepping aside for them.

She laid her hand over his name. 'I wish we'd had the chance to know each other, Dad. But maybe I'll get to know you more through your mum.'

The Queen.

Who was waiting for Louisa in the cathedral...with Sébastien. The man who'd suggested that she could marry him. Not 'should', but 'could'. Suggesting, rather than ordering. It still rankled that he'd said it. But Sébastien Moreau was the kind of person who thought deeply about things before he spoke. The kind of person it was worth listening to.

Just…marriage?

'I'm sticking to my decision, Dad,' she said softly. 'Doing what you did. Marrying for love, or not at all.'

She took a photograph of the grave for her grandmother, then headed out to where the Queen and Sébastien were sitting.

'Are you all right, Louisa?' Sébastien asked gently.

Although he hadn't touched her or even moved towards her, weirdly it felt as if he'd just given her a hug. Even more weirdly, she was tempted to walk into his arms, rest her head on his shoulder, and take strength from his nearness.

So not appropriate, given that he'd proposed a marriage of convenience.

She dragged her mind back to her present situation. 'I'm fine, thanks.' She turned to the Queen. 'Thank you for letting me see the grave and put a rose there.' Even if it was tidied away again by the cathedral staff in a few minutes' time, at least she'd been able to put the rose on his grave for her mum.

'I wish he'd had the chance to meet you,' Marguerite said. 'And I'm sorry your mother didn't…' Her words tailed off, but Louisa was pretty sure she knew what the Queen meant.

Breaking protocol, she took Marguerite's hand and squeezed it. 'I understand.'

Back at the palace, Sébastien excused himself to catch up on paperwork and Louisa thoroughly enjoyed spending the rest of the morning with her grandmother, looking through photographs of her father as a child and listening to Marguerite's stories. Though she also found herself wondering what Sébastien had been like as a child: had he been quiet and serious, as he was now? As the second of four boys, had he grown up in a big, noisy family full of laughter—the way she had, even though she was an only child?

Not that it was any of her business.

She showed the Queen photographs of herself as a small child and gave her copies of the wedding photographs.

'New York.' Marguerite looked at the photographs and took a deep breath. 'I always thought he'd marry here, in the cathedral where all the Princes of Charlmoux were christened and married. I thought I'd see him get married.'

'Nan always regretted not being able to make Mum's wedding dress,' Louisa said. 'She made the wedding dresses for all my aunts and cousins. And she'll definitely make mine.'

'So you have a young man back in London?'

'No.' Louisa smiled ruefully. 'Nobody's ever

made me feel the way my dad made my mum feel. I'll know when I meet the right one.'

'Hmm,' the Queen said.

'It's all right,' Louisa reassured her. 'Sébastien will find a way to work this out so nothing will change here. He'll step up to the throne at the end of the summer, as planned, and I'll be back in London.'

'Maybe,' Marguerite said. 'The DNA test might change everything.'

Louisa shook her head. 'My father was a prince—though I still can't quite get my head round that. But I'm not a princess or a queen, and I belong in London. Though I hope,' she said, 'that you and I will stay in touch.'

'We will,' the Queen said warmly.

Marguerite persuaded Louisa to stay for lunch with her, and asked Sébastien to join them. 'Perhaps you could show Louisa round the palace, this afternoon,' she suggested.

'That's kind, but we have an appointment with the curators at the Museum of Charlmoux, *madame*,' Sébastien said. 'They're letting us see exhibits that aren't often on show that I think Louisa might be interested in—a wedding dress from the eighteenth century, and some things called *marquettes*.'

'Samplers,' Louisa said. 'Although they're decorative nowadays, back then they were functional. They taught girls their alphabet and how to embroider for their trousseau.' She smiled. 'You might regret this, Sébastien. I can talk for hours about fabric and needlecraft technique. You'll probably have to tell me to shut up.'

'Indeed,' he said dryly. But there was a flicker of amusement in his eyes. She realised that he was laughing with her rather than at her, and it warmed her.

Once they'd left the Queen, they both changed into casual clothes.

Seeing Sébastien Moreau in jeans for the first time made her catch her breath; he looked even more gorgeous than he did in a suit. For the first time, he looked accessible. *Touchable*. His plain blue T-shirt hinted at a perfect six-pack beneath; he'd teamed it with faded denims and plain black trainers.

'I didn't expect you to wear jeans,' she said. 'I didn't think you'd even own any.'

He smiled. 'The idea is to blend in with the rest of the tourists. And of course I have jeans. Do you really think I'd go grape-picking in a suit?'

'You go grape-picking?' she asked, surprised.

'The whole family joins in at harvest time,' he said. 'I always take a fortnight off to help.'

She could just imagine it: his family, working together, chattering and laughing, then eating together at a long table spread with a red-and-white-checked cloth in the evening. So very different from the starched, formal life at the palace.

But this was his choice—and she had no right to judge him, she reminded herself.

Pierre joined them, also in casual clothing, strolling just far enough away to give them privacy yet near enough to make sure that Sébastien was safe. Louisa didn't think she'd ever get used to the idea of having personal security.

The museum was a pale stone building with tall windows and a slate roof; next to the river, it looked very pretty indeed, and she took a few snaps to send to her family later. If he'd asked her beforehand about her idea of the perfect afternoon, it would've been this: in a museum, with a private viewing of historical textiles and talking to a curator who knew her subject inside-out. The eighteenth-century wedding dress, the *marquettes* and the Regency era shoes all fascinated her.

Louisa loved the fact that Sébastien had made the effort to find something she'd enjoy. He was quietly thoughtful, a quality she appreciated.

But then again, he'd also suggested a marriage of convenience. She still couldn't quite believe he'd done that, and she was cross with herself for letting it stick in her head. They'd known each other for less than a week. Marriage was completely out of the question.

Even if she did think he was gorgeous.

Even if he did pay attention to what she said.

Even if he did intrigue her.

He was really patient in the museum, translating when either Louisa or the curator got stuck; even though it clearly wasn't something that interested him, he didn't press them to rush and didn't seem to mind that their appointment overran by quite a big margin.

Once they'd finished at the museum, he bought them both iced coffees and showed her the pretty tourist spots round the city, everything from an iconic bridge with love locks clasped to it through to pretty squares, a gorgeous glass arcade, and the fountain outside the city hall.

Charlmoux was a beautiful country, but it was odd to think that her father had grown up here—that, had the accident not happened, she might have grown up here. Yet it didn't feel like home; it felt so very far away from London.

There had been no communication from the Queen, so Séb was pretty sure that there wouldn't be a summons to join the royal table for dinner. But that gave him the chance to show Louisa a side of the palace he liked, and maybe change her view of life as a royal. 'Perhaps you'd like to have dinner with me this evening, and then I can show you the palace gardens?'

'That would be nice.'

Polite mode. Well, he could change that. Surprise her. 'Good. We'll stop at the supermarket on the way back.'

She frowned. 'Don't you have to eat whatever the palace kitchens cook?'

'Only if it's a formal dinner and I'm attending,' he said. 'Otherwise, it's my choice. And, actually, cooking relaxes me.'

'Then I hope you'll let me help.'

Working with her would be a way of showing her that they could be a good team. 'Sure.' It had been a while since he'd shopped for himself—with his timetable, it was easier to have groceries delivered—and he was surprised by how much he enjoyed the domesticity of it. Back at his flat, between them they prepared Parmentier potatoes, salmon baked with a pesto crust, greens that he was going to wilt in garlic butter, and apple crumble made the way her grandmother had taught her, with cinnamon and oats.

'And a glass of wine while it's all cooking,' he said, taking a bottle of rosé from the fridge. 'This is from my family's vineyard. I hope you don't mind your rosé on the dry side.'

'Perfect for a summer evening,' she said.

He poured them both a glass and handed one to her, then raised his in a toast. 'Welcome to Charlmoux.'

'Thank you.' She took a sip. 'This is seriously nice.'

'Thank you. I'll pass your comments back to Luc.'

'He's your brother in charge of the vineyard?'

Séb nodded. 'He has twin girls who currently spend their days dressed as fairies, complete with wings and magic wands.'

She laughed. 'I remember going through that phase. Nan had this amazing shimmery material, all ice blue and silver. She made me the perfect dress and gauzy wings.'

He could imagine it. And all of a sudden he could see Louisa with her own daughter on her lap, reading fairy stories together. A daughter—*their* daughter—in a fairy dress, waving a magic wand…

He shook himself, and brought the conversation back to something much less dangerous for his peace of mind.

Dinner was perfect. Louisa insisted on sharing the washing up; her bare arm brushed accidentally against Séb's and his blood felt as if it was fizzing through his veins. He needed to be careful here. If he lost his head and gave in to the crazy impulse to wrap her in his arms and kiss her, he'd make a mess of this. Her time here had nothing to do with attraction; it was about doing the right thing for Charlmoux. As Louis' daughter, she was the rightful heir. Blocking her accession to the throne would be a huge miscarriage of justice.

'Come and see the gardens,' he said.

They walked together in the dappled evening sunlight. The rose garden was in full bloom, richly scented, and the herbaceous borders were a riot of colour and shapes.

'This is gorgeous,' she said. 'Is it open to the public?'

'No,' he said, 'but that might be a consideration for the future.'

'Beauty like this needs to be shared,' she said. 'Even if it's only a couple of days a week. It's too lovely to be kept to just a few people.'

He liked the generosity of her spirit. 'You're right,' he agreed. The security team would raise a few objections, but they wouldn't be insurmountable. 'Is that what you'd do? Open it a couple of days a week?'

She nodded. 'Either with no admission charge, or a small one that would go to an appropriate charity. Granddad's involved with a scheme that helps disabled people visit gardens. He's talked a few people into opening their private gardens a couple of times a year to help. My cousins and I—and Nan and my aunts—bake the cakes for afternoon tea to raise more funds.'

Given how excellent her apple crumble had been, he wasn't surprised that she could bake. 'What's your speciality?' he asked.

'Lemon drizzle,' she said. 'I always used to make it with Nan's recipe, but when my best friend went vegan I found a good recipe with no eggs or dairy so she didn't miss out. We make sure there's a gluten-free option among the cakes, too, so everyone's included.'

The way she'd been brought up sounded very much like the way he'd been brought up. 'My mum always baked for school fundraisers,' he said. 'Madeleines and lemon tarts.' His mother would adore Louisa. Not that it should matter: he'd made it clear to his family that when he eventually got married it would be a dynastic match, not for love. To someone who could cope with living in the public eye. Now, Séb was starting to wonder whether he'd made the right decision. He'd planned to marry for duty; Louisa was adamant that she'd only marry for the kind of love her parents had shared. But could there be a middle way?

The walled kitchen garden was next, and he showed her the heritage varieties they'd gathered over the last five years.

'Granddad would love this,' she said. 'He adores his allotment. If he was here he'd make a beeline for the head gardener and ask if they could swap some seeds.'

'I can arrange that, if you know what he'd like,' he said.

'Can I take some photographs for him and talk to him about it?'

'Sure,' he said. 'Though obviously I'd ask you to bear in mind security issues.' He wasn't going to be heavy-handed about it; Louisa was bright enough to see the issues for herself.

'Of course. Maybe you'd like to check the photographs before I send them,' she said. 'Do you walk here much?'

'Every evening, if I'm here and there isn't a function,' he said. 'I like walking here first thing in the morning, too, when it's just me and the birds singing their heads off. It reminds me of home.' He hadn't intended to let that slip out. In future, he'd need to be more careful; this wasn't about opening his own heart.

'It's hard to believe we're in the middle of a huge city,' she said. 'This feels like the middle of the countryside.'

He took her through a side gate to the formal knot garden with the fountain at its centre.

'I love this,' she said. She bent to sniff the

lavender, then glanced up at him and smiled. 'I might ask the Queen if I can take a cutting.'

Séb wondered if she had any idea just how beautiful she was. Then he caught his thoughts; this wasn't about attraction, it was about a sensible business arrangement. About joining forces with the woman who was the biological heir to the throne, so his last decade's work wasn't wasted and the country would be guided safely.

Living in a flat meant having no garden. Even Louisa's grandparents' garden, although full of flowers, was tiny; her grandfather grew all the veg at his allotment. Having a garden like this to walk through every day, winding down from work, must be utter bliss, she thought. The colours, the shapes, the birdsong, the splash of water in the fountain…just *bliss*.

Walking here with Sébastien, she could imagine this was their own private paradise: from the formal knot garden with its neat hedges of box and lavender, through to the lushness of the rose garden and then the bursts of colour in the borders.

It was incredibly romantic, filling all her senses.

Her hand accidentally brushed against his, and a tingle shot straight up her arm. It would be oh, so easy to let her fingers tangle with Sébastien's and walk hand in hand with him in the peace of the palace gardens. Maybe kiss him in one of the rose arbours...

But they weren't dating. They weren't falling in love with each other. Sébastien might be gorgeous, and thoughtful, and have all the qualities she'd want in a partner: but they weren't really on the same side. He'd suggested marriage as a business arrangement, and Louisa refused to marry for any reason other than love.

The tiny personal bits he'd let slip—about his nieces and his mother's baking—made her think that Sébastien was the kind of man she could fall in love with. But there was a crown in the way, and she needed to keep that in mind.

Once they were back in the corridor outside their apartments, she smiled at him. 'Thank you for today. I really enjoyed the museum. Showing me round must've put you very behind with your admin, so I won't take up any more of your time today.'

He gave a formal half-bow. 'I'm glad you enjoyed it. And you must be tired.'

They both knew she wasn't.

But she could see in his eyes that he, too, thought it would be safer to spend the rest of the evening apart—putting themselves out of reach of a temptation that would seriously complicate things.

'*À demain,*' she said.

'*À demain,*' he echoed. 'I'll see you for breakfast, and then we can plan what you'd like to do for the rest of the day.'

'All right. Would you mind just checking my photographs, first, to make sure there aren't any security issues?'

'Of course.' He took her phone and skimmed through the photos she'd taken of the garden. 'They're all fine.'

Back in her apartment, she sent texts to her family to show them the *marquettes* and the wedding dress, and the bits of the palace gardens she thought they'd love. Then she soaked in the bath and thought about Sébastien. He was still almost as much of an enigma now as he'd been the first day she'd met him in London. She knew a little about his family, and she knew he had integrity.

But did a man so schooled to duty have any room in his heart for love? Because, without love, there was no way she could consider marrying him.

CHAPTER SIX

ON SUNDAY MORNING, after breakfast, Sébastien showed Louisa round the palace.

'The Queen has requested that we have lunch with her,' he said, 'and maybe this afternoon I can drive you out to see some of the countryside. Maybe I can show you the lavender fields.'

'Thank you. I'd like that,' she said.

She was just taking a closer look at a wall-hanging in one of the large reception rooms when she heard Sébastien give a sharp intake of breath. 'Good morning, *sire.*'

Seer. There was only one person he could possibly be addressing. A person with a slow, measured tread interspersed by a tap.

Her grandfather.

Adrenalin shivered through her.

'*Madame* has given me permission to show Miss Gallet some of the rooms in the palace,' Sébastien continued. '*Sire*, may I present Miss Louisa Gallet?'

She turned round to face him, glad that Sébastien was standing right next to her.

'Miss Gallet,' the King said, his voice cool.

'Louisa, this is King Henri IV of Charlmoux.'

Curtsey. Louisa knew she ought to curtsey. But the contempt in the King's expression made her fold her arms and glare straight back at him. *'Sire.'*

'The dancer's daughter,' the King mused, a sneer on his lip.

'Prima ballerina,' she corrected, just about managing to keep her voice cool and collected. How dare this man disparage her mother? 'A position which I'm sure you realise only comes through talent and a lot of hard work. My mother was amazing, both as a ballerina and as a person, and I'm very proud of her. I'm proud of where I come from.' But she couldn't help adding waspishly, 'I know you come from a privileged background, but surely you can appreciate the value of determination and effort? Or are you just as snobbish with Sébastien because he doesn't come from a background like yours?'

'Leave it there, Louisa,' Sébastien murmured to her. 'Confrontation isn't going to help.'

She knew that, and she would've managed to keep her temper under control had the King not curled his lip at her. 'It seems you are an insubordinate child.'

'Child?' She scoffed. 'You're almost a decade away from teenage me, and you're fifteen years away from the lippy twelve-year-old I once was.'

The King frowned. 'Lippy?'

'*Insolente,*' Sébastien translated.

'But then, I didn't know you existed,' she said. She lifted her chin. 'Whereas I rather think you knew about me.'

The King fixed her with a steely glare. She glared back, standing her ground; and the King was the first to look away.

Then she noticed that the hand leaning on the stick was trembling. She remembered what Sébastien had said about the King being ill. And maybe, just maybe, the King's confrontational manner was because he couldn't bear to admit to what he saw as weakness and anyone else would see as understandable: grief and loss.

She'd been at that place where you'd just lost the person you loved most in the world, and everything felt as if it had caved in on top of you.

Even though she was still angry about the way he'd behaved towards her mother, she could empathise with his loss. Having a fight with him now wasn't going to make a scrap of difference to the past. They needed to find a point of agreement rather than stoke the discord between them.

She could feel Sébastien move beside her; he was clearly about to try mediating, but she wanted to do this herself. She held up one hand as a signal to him.

Still looking at the King, she said, '*Sire*, it must be as hard for you and the Queen, losing your only child, as it was for my grandparents to lose their only daughter. As it was for me to lose the only parent I knew. And I'm sorry I didn't get the chance to know your son. Everything my mother and my grandparents told me about him, everything the Queen told me yesterday, makes me know I would have loved him. Just as I know he would have loved me.'

The King looked back at her; he didn't say a word, and she knew he was giving her the chance to put her side of things.

'I haven't come here to tarnish your son's memory, *sire*,' she said quietly. 'Far from it. I'm here to do the DNA test and to learn more about the side of my life I didn't know about before. And maybe it's a chance for you to learn more about the side of his life that you—' She stopped. The King *had* known about his son's marriage. And she wasn't prepared to pretend that the King had been left in the dark. She finished with the nearest she could get to a compromise. 'That you weren't as familiar with. I have given the Queen some photographs, and

I'd be happy to answer any questions you might have.'

The King looked at her some more. Then he inclined his head. 'We will speak later.' With that he turned away and walked out of the room, leaning on his cane but keeping his back straight.

Louisa blew out a breath. 'That was…' She had no words to describe it.

'It could've been a lot worse,' Sébastien said. 'Shouting—'

'—doesn't make things better,' she cut in. 'I know. I'm sorry. I didn't mean to start a fight.'

'Sure you're really fifteen years away from being a lippy twelve-year-old?' His smile took the sting out of his words; and he was right. They did need to laugh about it and break the strain.

'I might've regressed a bit.' She rolled her eyes. 'Which is atrocious of me. I'm usually really good with Mumzillas.'

'Mumzillas?' He tilted his head to one side, his dark eyes holding hers.

'Difficult mothers of the bride—the sort who micromanage and go over the top,' she said. 'I can normally talk them round. Perhaps I should try to see the King as a Mumzilla.' She spread her hands. 'A Kingzilla, maybe.'

Sébastien burst out laughing. 'Just don't ever tell him that's what you think of him.'

'Now I've said it, it's going to be very hard not to,' she said.

'What you said to him—that was kind,' Sébastien said.

'I was trying to empathise with him. It doesn't stop me being angry about his behaviour,' she said, 'but understanding is the first step to finding compromise. I'm not here to fight.'

'I'm glad to hear it,' he said dryly. 'So—on with the tour?'

'On with the tour,' she said. It was strange how relaxed she felt in Sébastien's company. As if she'd always known him. She felt *settled* when she was with him; and, considering they'd only known each other for a few days, that was strange.

At lunch, the King was notable by his absence, but Louisa chattered happily to the Queen about her visit to the museum and what she thought of the palace tapestries. She wasn't sure whether the Queen knew she'd clashed with the King or whether Marguerite was being tactful and not discussing it, but she was starting to really like her other grandmother.

Sébastien took her out to see the lavender fields after lunch.

'You're allowed to drive?' she asked, surprised, when he opened the front passenger door for her and then climbed in behind the wheel while Pierre sat in the back.

'Provided I have security with me, yes,' he said.

'Even when you visit your family?'

'Pierre's an honorary Moreau,' he said. 'He's getting very good at picking grapes; though he's not as good as me at backing up a tractor and trailer.'

She laughed. 'Right.'

The lavender fields were stunning against the bright blue Mediterranean sky, swathes of purple bordered by bright yellow cornfields and tall dark green cypress trees. Sébastien parked the car so they could walk along the edge of one of the fields, and Louisa took plenty of photographs to send home, knowing how much her grandparents would enjoy them. Her mother would've loved visiting here; Louisa could just imagine her mother dancing between the rows of lavender bushes while her father watched, smiling.

'OK?' Sébastien asked.

'Just thinking about my parents and imagining them here,' she said.

He took her hand and squeezed it briefly. 'I'm sorry. I didn't mean to make you sad.'

'I'm not sad, exactly.'

'Douce-amère,' he said. 'Bittersweet.'

'Yes. It's the things you didn't get a chance to do that you miss,' she said softly.

He didn't release her hand as they continued walking, and it made her feel cherished. She'd remember this moment for ever: walking in the warmth of the sun, with the scent of lavender surrounding them, birds singing, and Sébastien holding her hand.

Sébastien was the kind of man who noticed little things, and knew what to do to make things feel better. And he did it quietly, without making a fuss: she appreciated that. More than that, it made her think again about his proposal. He'd made it sound like a business deal; but holding someone's hand to comfort them wasn't businesslike. It was personal.

Was it the right solution to their dilemma?

Could he grow to love her? Were these weird feelings bubbling through her the beginning of falling in love with him?

She had no answers, and she wasn't ready to discuss it. But Sébastien was just there, holding her hand, not demanding or pushing. Just *there*. And, right at that moment, she was glad.

Séb had meant to hold Louisa's hand simply to give her a moment of comfort. But, for the life of him, he couldn't release her hand. Not when the lavender bloomed in front of them, scenting the air. Not when the birds were singing. Not when the sun kissed their skin.

He'd never felt like this before, and it worried him. He needed to keep a clear head to sort out the accession to the throne. But being with Louisa made him feel giddy. He needed to pay attention and focus on his duty.

Just as they got back to the car, Pascal called. Séb sighed at the news. 'Pierre, would you mind driving us back?'

'Of course,' the security detail said with a smile.

'What's happened?' Louisa asked, climbing into the back of the car with him.

He brought one of the press websites up on his phone and passed it to her so she could see the headline: *Who's That Girl?* The photograph was of them together after the ballet, and below that was another of them at the museum.

She blanched. 'Does that mean they'll find out who I am and start talking about the throne?'

'Apologies for sounding arrogant, but they're probably focused on me,' Sébastien said, 'and the story will be about whether you're a candidate for a future bride.' He sighed. 'They do this whenever they spot me with anyone female. It's one of the reasons I don't date very much, because it puts too much pressure on my girlfriend.' Pressure that had shattered his relationship with Elodie beyond any hope of repair.

'But I'm not your girlfriend,' she pointed out.

The air suddenly felt as tight as a coiled spring. She wasn't his girlfriend. *But what if...?*

'No,' he said, 'you're not. Don't worry. It'll die down.' He hoped. And he hoped these weird, unexpected feelings would die down, too. There was no place for feelings where the throne was concerned.

There was no summons from the King when they returned to the palace, and the Queen was conspicuous by her absence, too. Séb made a few enquiries. 'The King isn't well,' he told Louisa.

'Is it my fault?' she asked.

'No.' Although the tension earlier probably hadn't helped matters with the King's health, he wasn't going to dump that particular burden on her. 'I'm afraid you're stuck with me or your own company, this evening.'

'Do you need to work?'

'No.' Which wasn't strictly true, but he could catch up later. 'We could walk in the gardens again.'

'I'd like that,' she said.

Although Séb kept the conversation light between them, he was still thinking of how he'd felt in the lavender fields. He felt it here, too; he could imagine her barefoot on the lawn, teaching two children to throw a tennis ball for the dogs—just as his own mother had taught him.

Oh, help.

Fantasising about a future with Louisa wasn't a good idea. He didn't want her to feel forced into marrying him. Suddenly, he wanted her to want to be with him. And his plans for a marriage of convenience simply imploded.

Clearly the media had been doing some digging overnight, because Monday's newspapers had a new headline—*Our Secret Princess!*—and she learned from Sébastien that the staff at the palace press office were kept busy firefighting.

'Can I leave you to your own devices?' Sébastien asked. 'You're welcome to sit in my office with a book or what have you, but there are going to be a lot of phone calls.'

'All in French, using vocab I didn't have to start with, and at a speed where I can't pick out the words,' she said. 'I think I'd rather stay here in the quiet and sew.'

'All right. If there's anything you need, text me,' he said.

Louisa lost herself in her embroidery, but late that morning there was a knock on her door. When she answered, it was one of the liveried footmen; he spoke excellent English which put her French to shame. 'Mademoiselle Gallet, *madame* requests your company. Would you come with me?'

She left her sewing where it was and followed him to the Queen's drawing room. He had a rapid conversation with the liveried footman at the door, who announced her. But when she walked in, she discovered the King and Sébastien waiting with the Queen.

'Thank you for coming, Louisa,' Marguerite said. 'Please sit down.'

Heart thumping, Louisa took a seat on the sofa next to Sébastien, opposite the King and Queen. She caught Sébastien's eye and he mouthed something at her; it took her a moment to work out that it was *Kingzilla*. She managed to stop herself bursting into laughter, but he'd made her relax in the best possible way.

'The lab results are back,' Sébastien said.

'Already?' She frowned. 'I thought you said it would take three days?'

'They've been working intensely to speed things up a bit,' he said. 'Which is just as well, given the press at the moment.'

'And?' For pity's sake, this wasn't like some televised awards do where the presenter had been briefed to give a massive dramatic pause before announcing the winner. She needed to know the truth. *Now.*

'There are enough points of similarity be-tween your test and those of *madame* and *sire* to say with certainty that you are Louis' daughter.'

She glanced at the King, who had gone puce but was silent.

Unexpectedly, Marguerite stood up and walked over to her. 'I knew when I met you on Friday that you were my granddaughter. Now we have the scientific proof.'

Louisa stood up and hugged her.

'And now I can welcome you to Charlmoux properly, *ma petite-fille*.'

'Isn't that "little girl"?' Louisa asked.

'*Fille* is daughter, *petite-fille* is granddaugh-ter,' Marguerite explained. 'And maybe one day you'll come to call me *mémère*.'

'I assume that's French for "grandma"?'

Marguerite nodded. 'Or *mémé*, for a pet name, but I know I need to earn that.' She hugged Lou-isa again. 'I am so glad. I miss your father very much and now I will get to see him again in you.' She glanced at the King. 'And when Henri steps down at the end of the summer, you will be Queen.'

'Forgive me for being blunt, but I'm *not* a queen,' Louisa said. 'I know what I've read about Charlmoux and what Sébastien has told me, but I'm English. My life is in London—my family, my friends, my job. I'm not pushing you away, and I'm very glad to have my father's family as part of my life, but there's no way I can be Queen of Charlmoux. Sébastien is the heir. There's the Act of Parliament in place.'

'That's superseded by your existence,' Marguerite said. 'Isn't it, Sébastien?'

'I think,' Sébastien said, 'I need to take Louisa somewhere out of the way of the press until we're absolutely clear about the situation.'

'Where will you take her? To your family?' the Queen asked.

'I was thinking perhaps the summer palace,' Sébastien said, 'but obviously that would be with your permission and provided schedules allow.'

'That's a good idea. I'll get Emil onto it and he can move anything necessary,' Marguerite said.

'Who's Emil?' Louisa asked.

'The King's PA, like Pascal is mine,' Sébastien explained.

'Do I get any say in this?' Louisa asked. 'My vote would be to put me on a plane back to London.'

'And abandon you to the media?' Séb asked. 'No. Being doorstepped can feel overwhelming. We need to protect you, work out what we'll say to the press, and look at what additional skills you need.'

Louisa looked at the King, who had been silent throughout and clearly wasn't happy about the results of the DNA test at all. 'I don't think you would like me to be Queen, either, *sire*. Which puts us on the same side.'

'It's a shambles,' he said, shaking his head. 'You can't stay here, because the press will be at the gates. And you can't go back to London, because they'll hound you. Sébastien is right.' He pursed his lips. 'Go to the summer palace.'

'But won't the press follow us there?'

'The press are very used to anonymous cars with darkened windows coming and going from the palace,' Sébastien said. 'They'll assume that I'm going somewhere, or that we're sending a car to pick someone up for a meeting here. They won't know you're in the car, and we won't be tailed. Pierre will act as your security detail as well as mine. If you pack your things now, we'll leave before lunch. Anything else you need, we can order on the way.'

'But—'

'No buts, *ma petite-fille*,' Marguerite said. 'We'll look after you.'

'Don't worry about work back in London,' Sébastien said. 'You told me last week that you could make any time this week—your cousins are handling your clients at the bridal workshop, and your boss gave you time off from the Heritage Centre. We should have this all sorted by the end of the week.'

That long? she thought, dismayed.

'Bridal workshop,' the King muttered, and rolled his eyes.

Louisa narrowed her eyes at him. 'I'm very good at my job, as you'd know if you'd actually bothered to take an interest.'

'Henri, stop it,' Marguerite said firmly. 'And, Louisa, just because your grandfather snipes at you, it doesn't mean you have to snipe back. Be the better person.'

Louisa had never seen a king being told off before—or been told off herself by a queen. And she knew that Marguerite was right. This was exactly how Veronica would've handled the same kind of situation if Jack had clashed with any of his children or grandchildren. 'Sorry, *madame*,' she said. At Marguerite's piercing gaze, she added, 'I apologise, *sire*.'

'Henri?' Marguerite looked at the King.

'*Pardon,*' he muttered, then rolled his eyes and added, 'Louisa.'

'*Bien.*' Marguerite gave a sharp nod. 'Now, Sébastien. You were saying?'

'Louisa,' he continued, 'you can stay for another week, if need be. That will give us enough time to work out how we're going to handle the situation and for me to assess what skills you have already and what I need to teach you.'

'But I don't want to be qu...' Her voice tailed off as she registered the grimness of his expression.

'It isn't a matter of choice any more, I'm afraid,' he said.

'If the King can stand down, why can't I?' she asked. 'Surely now we've proved who I am, I can renounce the crown.'

'I'm working on it,' he said, 'but we need to be prepared for all eventualities.'

All eventualities. Did that include marrying him? If he raised the issue now, in front of the King and Queen...

To her relief, instead he asked, 'How long will it take you to pack?'

'Ten minutes,' Louisa said.

'Good organisation skills. That's an excellent start,' he said. 'I'll show you back to your apartment.'

By the time she'd packed and knocked on his apartment door, he'd packed, too. They returned to the drawing room so she could say goodbye to the Queen.

'Stay in touch, *ma petite*,' Marguerite said.

'*Oui, madame.*'

Louisa was about to curtsey when Marguerite added, 'And don't you dare curtsey to me. You're my granddaughter.'

Louisa smiled and gave her a hug instead.

'You curtsey to me. I'm the King,' Henri said, his chin jutting out obstinately.

'Yes, you are,' Louisa said. 'But you're also my grandfather. Tell me, *sire*, do you plan on being the same kind of grandparent that you were a father-in-law?'

'Insolente,' the King said, scowling.

'I'll hold my tongue,' Louisa said. 'Solely for my grandmother's sake.'

He scowled even harder.

She didn't curtsey to him; but he didn't hug her. Stalemate it was, then.

'Au revoir,' she said.

'Bonne journée,' the Queen said. 'Look after her, Sébastien.'

She insisted on carrying her own luggage to the car, and noticed that he did the same. He held the door to let her into the back seat of the car first, then joined her.

'So what now? Do I hide my face as we go out of the gates?' she asked as Pierre took the wheel.

'There's no need,' Sébastien reassured her. 'The car has privacy glass, so they won't be able to see in.'

'It feels as if we're rushing down a rollercoaster slope and I can't stop the car,' she said.

'I understand,' he said. 'I felt the same, the first time the paparazzi looked for me, but you get used to it.'

'I don't want to get used to it, Sébastien,' she said. 'I'm not a princess.'

'Technically,' he said, 'you are, and I should be calling you *madame*.'

'Oh, *puh-lease*,' she said, rolling her eyes. 'You first knew me as plain Louisa Gallet. That's not going to change just because…' She closed her eyes for a moment.

'Everything's changed,' he said softly. And there was nothing plain about her. Nothing at all. She glowed from the inside out.

She opened her eyes again. 'Technically, do you have to bow to me?'

He stifled his amusement. Just. 'Yes.'

'Well, *don't*,' she said. 'I'm not a princess.'

Yes, she was, but she clearly needed time to get used to it. 'All right, plain Mademoiselle Louisa. Let's get to work,' he said. 'I'm going to make notes as we talk, if that's all right.' He smiled at her. 'Talk me through what happens between someone making an appointment and you giving them the finished dress.'

'How much detail do you want?' she asked.

'As much as you want to give,' he said.

'OK. I ask them to bring their ideas to the appointment—any pictures they've seen of dresses they like, the sort of colour scheme they're thinking about, the sort of hairstyle and veil and bouquet they want. We talk about what she likes, and we have gowns she can try on to see how it looks.' She ticked off the steps on her fingers. 'That's the point where I might guide her towards a different-shaped gown, one that'll flatter her shape better and will make her feel fabulous. Then we'll go through the material samples so she chooses the type of material and colour. I'll make a trial dress in very light cotton, and we'll agree any changes in hemline or shape or decoration. Then I cut out the real material and pin it together, do a fitting, sew it and add the decoration, do another fitting with the shoes and underwear she'll wear on the day to make sure it all works, pin up any final alterations, and then it's the final fitting where she takes the dress away.'

'In business terms, you break the task into steps, you know which order each step has to be done in, and you work your way through it.'

She nodded.

'And all the time you deal with your clients—and their families—you need to take their feelings into account.'

'Yes.'

'It's exactly the same with being a royal,' he

said. 'Just your projects might be a bit different. So you're not actually as under-prepared as you think. You already have some skills—organisation and diplomacy for a start. What media experience do you have?'

'I've been interviewed a couple of times,' she said, 'mainly by the local paper and specialist bridal magazines and websites. I've also talked to specialist heritage websites about my restoration work.'

'Then you already know some of the media skills,' he said. 'It'll be just a matter of practising and polishing.'

'I don't want to do this at all,' she said.

He took her hand and squeezed it. 'I'm trying to find an escape route for you, Louisa, but you need to understand that it might not be possible.'

'Can't I be like a...like a sleeping partner?' she asked plaintively.

Oh, the picture that put in his head. Of waking in the morning with her in his arms, her head pillowed on his shoulder. Of her smiling at him when she opened her eyes. Of her reaching up to kiss him good morning, and kissing would turn to touching...

Louisa saw the deep slash of colour across Sébastien's cheekbones and realised how her comment must have sounded to him.

'I meant in business terms,' she mumbled.

But it was too late; there was a picture in her head, too. Of Sébastien sprawled across her bed. He clearly had a similar picture in his head, because his fingers tightened round hers for a moment.

'Business terms,' he said, obviously making an effort. 'Business. OK. There is a way, but you've already said no to that.'

She grimaced. 'I can't marry you just to get out of ruling the country.'

'We both win, that way,' he said.

'What if you fall in love with someone? What if I fall in love with someone?'

'Then you'd have to suppress it. To be royal is to put the country first,' he said.

She shook her head in exasperation. 'That's so cold-blooded.'

'It's the way it is,' he said. 'The country needs stability.' His phone beeped; he glanced at the screen, then showed her the latest message from Pascal. 'The press have traced the same paper trail that I did. They've posted photographs of you and Louis, showing the similarity between you.'

'But they don't know the results of the DNA test.' And then a nasty thought hit her. 'Unless someone leaked it?'

'They don't need to know the results,' he said.

'Those headlines tell us they've already made up their minds. As far as they're concerned, you're the legitimate Princess of Charlmoux, and I'm no longer the legitimate heir. It's only a matter of time before they find out that's absolutely true.'

'But that's not fair on you. You've worked for the royal family for years, training to be a future king.' She bit her lip. 'I can't learn all that in a week.'

'No,' he agreed, 'but you can learn a lot.'

'I'm not going to be Queen.'

'If you step down, and I take over as Regent,' he said, 'what happens if you fall in love with someone, get married and have children? They'll still be next in line to the throne.'

'Not if you were King.'

'We're in uncharted territory,' he said gently. 'There is no precedent. Very few monarchs have abdicated, and only on the grounds of ill health. I might still be able to rule as your regent—if Parliament agrees—but *your* children would still be the heirs, not mine. So all you'd be doing is shifting the burden to them. Is that what you want?'

She simply stared at him.

'We can waste time arguing,' he said, 'or we can be practical. And you strike me as a practical woman.'

She narrowed her eyes at him. 'Are you trying to push me into marrying you?'

No. He was seeing everything he'd worked for about to go up in flames. Every sacrifice he'd made—losing his relationship with Elodie, not seeing enough of his family—would all be for nothing. And all his years of training, of looking at things calmly and dispassionately, had deserted him. He could feel the panic seeping through him like cold, stagnant water. What the hell was he going to do? How could he fix this?

He took a deep breath. 'No. I'm not trying to push you into marrying me. I'm telling you what your choices are.'

And only one of them included him. He pushed the thought away before it overwhelmed him. There was so much at stake here. 'Either you step up and rule the country—in which case I need to start getting you up to speed with things—or you marry me and let me rule, in which case I'll still need to teach you a few things because you'll still have to do at least some of the PR stuff.'

'I've already told you. The only reason I'll ever marry is the same as my parents. Love. Nothing less,' she said.

Even if you ignored the scientific proof, Séb thought, Louisa was Henri's granddaughter. She had the same obstinacy.

She wanted a fairy tale. True love.

The problem was, love *was* a fairy tale when it came to his world. There was no real room for love in a royal marriage. Mutual liking and respect would be a bonus, but the important thing was the ability to put the country first.

He couldn't give her any sweeteners. Maybe she'd feel better about the idea of getting married to him if she thought he was in love with her, or if she fell in love with him. But that would mean a combination of lying to her and manipulating her—neither of which sat well with him.

She was the heir, and he thought she had the makings of a good ruler. He just needed to teach her to see it, too.

'Let's get on with the business,' he said. 'There are royal duties. The diplomatic stuff: hosting foreign dignitaries and the like. The Queen will help with that, and the palace staff know what they're doing, but you still need to host people. And some of them can be difficult.' He smiled at her. 'Which is where your Mumzilla experience comes in.'

'Got it.'

'There's some legal work, but you'll be supported by the palace officials.'

She made another note on her phone.

'Then there are the charity patronships. Your

grandfather might want to keep some of them; your grandmother might want to keep others.'

'Are you a charity patron?' she asked.

He nodded. 'Mine are mainly to do with mental health and justice.'

'Because of what happened to your best friend?'

She'd remembered? Part of him felt warmed. 'Yes. The thing about a charity is to pick the ones you've got a personal connection with, either in your interests or your experience. I think you'd be particularly strong with heritage and the arts, because of your work and your mum. Plus bereavement—especially for children who've lost a parent.'

'Yes. And women's health and cancer, because of my mum,' she said. 'So what exactly does a charity patron do?'

'Your endorsement helps support awareness of the charity and raise their profile, which in turn helps them with fundraising. They might ask you to have your photograph on a leaflet, or help front an appeal,' he explained. 'You might be a keynote speaker, or turn up at an event as a VIP, or give out awards, or write something personal they can use in the press. It depends on what sort of involvement you want to have, and the palace press team can help you polish anything you're not sure about.'

'This all sounds quite daunting,' she said. 'I don't want to be Queen—and if it was a job I'd say that I wasn't a suitable candidate. I don't have the experience or the skills.'

'You're being too hard on yourself,' he said. 'Supposing someone joined the bridal workshop yesterday morning, you were assigned to be their mentor, and they told you at the end of their first day that they were rubbish at their job.'

She frowned. 'But that's ridiculous. Nobody can be perfect on day one. There's a lot to learn in the job, plus you need time to settle in.'

'Exactly.' Sébastien looked at her. 'You're not going to be the perfect princess right this very second. But you already have some of the skills from your job, and I can teach you the rest.'

'I'm not a princess,' she insisted. 'My life's in London.'

He spread his hands. 'Give me this week. See if it changes how you view things.'

'A week?' She bit her lip. 'I'll give you until Friday.'

He only had until Friday morning to teach her how to be a princess and step up to do the right thing.

But Sébastien had never shied away from a challenge, and he wasn't going to start now.

CHAPTER SEVEN

WHEN THEY ARRIVED at the royal summer palace, Sébastien showed Louisa to her room.

'I can see the sea!' she said, looking delighted. 'And it's actually turquoise, like the photographs. It's amazing.'

'We'll go for a walk on the beach, later,' he said. 'It's a private beach, and the locals are really protective of our privacy, so you don't have to worry about press intrusion.'

'That's good,' she said.

He showed her round, then introduced her to Hortense, the middle-aged housekeeper, who'd brewed coffee for them and had a tray with mugs, a cafetière and a jug of milk. 'We're going to take over the conservatory for our office, Hortense, if that doesn't get in your way?'

The housekeeper smiled. 'You never get in my way, Séb. Just let me know when you want more coffee.'

'We will.'

Louisa made the effort to thank Hortense in French, and the housekeeper patted her arm. *'De rien, ma petite.'* She smiled. 'I knew your *papa*. My mother was the housekeeper here before me, and your papa was very kind to a lonely little girl. He showed me how to make sandcastles on the beach, and make a bridge over the moat from razor shells.'

Séb could see the glint of tears in Louisa's eyes as she thanked Hortense.

'Everyone speaks well of your father,' he said gently as he ushered her to the conservatory. 'Louis was a good man.' And he rather thought that the people of Charlmoux would take Louisa to their hearts, too.

'The Queen showed me photographs of him at the beach. Would it have been here?' she asked.

'Very probably,' he said. 'OK. Time to make our game plan. I don't mean to scare you, but we need to be practical. Even if you can step down from royal duties—' and he was pretty sure that wasn't an option '—you'll still be of interest to the press and you'll need to be careful in public: what you do, what you say, and your expression.'

'Is that why you're always so starchy?'

It was the second time she'd accused him of that. 'I'm not starchy,' he said, stung.

'It's how you come across to me,' she said. 'I

have no idea what makes you tick. What makes you laugh, what makes you want to weep, what drives you.'

'In public,' he said, 'I've spent the last few years being the heir to the throne. The country needs me to be stable and serene—or, as you put it, starchy. I smile, I keep my shoulders relaxed and my head held high, and I smile some more.'

She frowned. 'It sounds like living in a goldfish bowl.'

'Yes,' he said. 'I'm afraid it goes with the territory. You get used to it.'

'I don't think I'd ever get used to it.' She grimaced. 'It was different for Mum; she was a performer. I'm more of a back room person.'

'The best performers are nervous before a show. Adrenalin keeps them sharp,' he said. 'Let's start with interviews. We'll role-play it, with me as the journalist, and film it on my laptop so we can review it together.'

'Like television, you mean?' Her eyes went wide. 'I've never done that.'

'I know,' he said, as gently as he could. 'We need to establish a baseline so we can see how you're coming across and what you need to work on.'

'Do you get questions in advance?'

'To some extent,' he said. 'The palace PR team will be well-briefed enough to come up with a list of the most likely questions in any given situation, so you'll be pretty much prepared. But you'll always get something you're not expecting.'

'Right.'

He patted her hand. 'This is a practice. A safe space, and there are no wrong answers,' he said. 'Go and sit on the sofa.' He started to set up his laptop. 'Most of this is obvious, but I'll give you a few tips while I'm getting the angle of the screen right. Smile and maintain eye contact—with your interviewer if it's in person, or with the camera if it's an online session.'

'Got it.'

'They'll want a good quote they can use, so keep your answer concise, clear and jargon-free; but also make sure you answer the question in full, because they might edit out the question if it's not a live broadcast. Focus on your key message. If you don't understand the question, ask for clarification. If you don't know the answer, say so, and say why—you might not have read a report, and it's better to say that rather than try to bluff your way through it. Speak slowly, keep it positive, and keep your speech to less than a minute at a time.'

'A minute's a very long time to talk,' she said.

'Exactly,' he said. 'Short and sweet is the way to go.'

'What if they ask me something I don't want to answer?'

'Use the ABC approach,' he said. 'Acknowledge the question, bridge your response, and contribute your key message.'

Louisa was glad that Sébastien was being brisk and businesslike with her. Of course the press were going to be interested in her, even if she did manage not to be on the throne, and it made sense to prepare herself as much as possible, to learn these new skills, she simply needed to pay attention and practise. 'ABC,' she repeated. 'Acknowledge, bridge, contribute.'

He came to sit next to her on the sofa. 'We're live now. Good afternoon, Your Highness. Thank you for joining me today.'

Highness? What? Then she remembered to smile and make eye contact. 'Thank you for inviting me, Mr Moreau.'

He gave her a predatory smile. 'How do you feel about becoming Queen?'

He wasn't even going to ask a soft question first, to let her warm up? Though maybe it was more realistic, because a journalist would go straight for the big one. ABC, she reminded herself. 'I can't really answer that properly at the moment, Mr Moreau,' she said, 'because that depends on whether there's someone more suitable to rule. But I'm very much looking forward to seeing more of Charlmoux and its people, including my father's parents.'

Sébastien gave her an approving wink, and whipped through his list of questions.

Louisa stumbled over a couple of the answers. 'Can we backtrack so you ask me the question again?' she asked.

'No. What would your mum have said to her students in a dress rehearsal?'

'Keep going and pick up your place as soon as you can,' she said.

'This is exactly the same thing. Ignore the mistakes and keep going,' he said. 'Smile. Make eye contact. Remember your key points. And we're back in role in three, two, one.'

The 'interview' only lasted for ten minutes, but it felt like much longer. By the end of it, Louisa felt as if someone had flattened her.

'Time to review it,' he said, and played back the recording.

Louisa was very aware of the way she'd messed up some of the answers. 'That really wasn't good,' she said when the recording stopped.

'It's a good *start*,' he corrected. 'Remember, this is our baseline and it'll get better from here on. What would you change for the next round?'

'I'd prepare the answers better, so I don't look

as if I'm making things up off the top of my head,' she said.

'That isn't being fair to yourself,' he said, 'because we didn't prepare in the first place. Don't change the goalposts.'

She knew he had a point; but seeing herself on screen, so gauche and hopeless, had rattled her. 'With your experience of giving interviews, what do you think I need to change first?' she asked.

'Your body language,' he said. 'You fidget with your hands, and fidgeting makes you look less confident.'

'How do I stop doing that?'

'When you're talking, use your hands,' he said.

She frowned. 'You just said I need to stop fidgeting with my hands. Doesn't using them mean I'm fidgeting?'

'No. When people talk normally,' he said, 'they tend to use their hands to emphasise points. Do that in an interview. Even if the camera's trained solely on your face, the gestures will make your face look more animated.'

She nodded. 'And when I'm not talking? How do I stop fidgeting?'

'Nest your hands together—one within the other—and keep them on your lap,' he said. 'It'll make you look relaxed, even if you're not feeling it.'

Louisa definitely wasn't feeling relaxed right then, but she followed his directions.

'And your posture,' he said. 'When you sit, lean forward slightly, with both feet on the floor; it's a more active position. If you're standing, put one foot slightly in front of the other and then you won't sway.'

'Is this better?' she asked, sitting in the way he'd suggested.

'Much,' he said. 'Last thing—shoulders relaxed and head high.'

She smiled. 'Mum used to tell me to pretend there's a string pulling me up from the top of my head. Long neck, shoulders down.'

'Perfect,' he said. 'That's probably why you walk like a dancer.'

He'd noticed that? It made her feel hot all over. Especially as she'd noticed how he moved, too, with economy and grace.

'Now we've done the physical stuff, let's go through your answers. You're doing most of the talking, and I'll make notes.'

He took her through each question, making her analyse her answers and consider where she thought they needed changing. By the time they'd finished, Louisa felt a lot more confident.

'Thank you. That was really useful,' she said. 'Let's repeat the interview and see how I'm doing.'

'We'll take a break, first,' Sébastien said. 'We've been focusing on this all afternoon. You need time to recharge and let this stuff sink into your brain. Let's go and walk by the sea. I'll just tell Pierre where we are.' He sent a message to his security detail, then shrugged off his jacket and removed his tie, and led her through the garden.

They left their shoes by the garden gate—the beach was sandy, studded every so often with shells and smooth pebbles—and headed down to the shoreline.

'I can't believe the colour of that water,' she said. 'Can I paddle, or do I have to be careful of jellyfish or what have you?'

'It's very safe,' he said. 'There might be the odd sharp shell, but that's it.' He rolled his trousers up to his knees. 'Come on.' He took her hand and drew her to the edge of the sea.

'Oh! It's colder than I expected,' she said. 'Do you come here often?'

'Not as often as I'd like,' he said. 'When I get time off, I tend to go and see my family. But the beach is a treat.'

'We sometimes went to Cornwall in the summer—Mum had some friends who moved there when they retired from dancing. I loved walking along the sea like this,' she said.

'Just you and the waves swishing onto the

shore. It's the best thing ever for clearing your head,' he said.

And then she realised that he was still holding her hand.

Suddenly this didn't feel like a break from business. It felt like a date. If she stood still and closed her eyes, would he kiss her? Would she taste the salt air on his lips? Would his kiss be sweet and offering, or hot and demanding?

She shook herself. This was ridiculous. And she couldn't let herself forget that he'd suggested a marriage of convenience. He only wanted to marry her for political reasons; letting herself get carried away by emotions would be very stupid. Even if it was the most beautiful summer day by the sea, and she was walking hand in hand with the most beautiful man.

She thought he was starchy. She didn't know what made him laugh, what made him weep, what drove him.

Séb had been so focused on wanting to change the world that he hadn't stopped to share his dreams with anyone. After Elodie, he'd thought that the kind of relationships the rest of his family had were out of his reach—that his eventual marriage would be a political match.

But was Louisa right? Could their match be more than just political?

If so, then she'd need him to open up to her; and he didn't even know how to start. He didn't open up to anyone nowadays—not even to his family and Marcel. He'd thought it was a strength, being self-contained; now, he wondered if it was a weakness.

Open up.

She'd told him what she didn't know about him. Maybe that would be the best place to start. 'Bad puns,' he said.

'What?'

'You asked what made me laugh. Bad puns,' he said.

'Uh-huh.' She looked wary, but intrigued as well.

'And my family. I laugh with my family. Especially my nieces, when they tell me a joke and get the punchline wrong. It's adorable.'

She smiled. 'Yeah. I'm dying for my cousins to start having babies, so I can read them the stories my mum read to me.'

Did she want babies of her own? The question caught in his throat and he couldn't ask her. 'Injustice,' he said instead. 'That's what makes me weep.'

'What actually happened to your best friend's family?' she asked.

He grimaced. 'It feels as if I'm betraying a confidence.'

'It's not going anywhere,' she said, tightening her fingers round his.

He knew he could trust her. So he told her.

'That's terrible,' she said when he'd finished. 'I was the same age as Marcel when I lost my mum. But she didn't want to die. It must be so much harder if you keep wondering why your dad would want to leave you—or if you could've said or done something to make a difference and stop him taking his own life, even when it's obvious that nobody could've changed what happened.'

'It's why I studied law,' he said. 'I wanted to help people who'd been through something like that. And I wanted to be able to change the law so there were more safeguards.'

'You said Marcel works with your brother Luc at the vineyard, now?'

He nodded. 'It was my suggestion. I felt bad about not being able to support him properly when it all happened. My parents were a bit wary at first. I mean, was a vineyard really the best place for someone who had a problem with alcohol? But I thought it would help because he'd be with people who valued him, and I hoped the job would make him focus on something physical and help stop things spinning round in his head. I couldn't help him as a teen, but I could help him when we were older, give

him the chance to get his life back on track.'
He shrugged. 'He's settled, now. He's getting
married after harvest, and I'm going to be his
best man.'

'I'm glad things have worked out for him,'
she said.

'So am I,' he said.

He found himself holding her hand until they
were back at the garden gate. And then, unable
to help himself, he drew her hand up to his lips,
pressed a kiss into her palm, then folded her fingers round it. 'Thank you for listening,' he said.

Her eyes had gone wide and colour had
bloomed in her cheeks.

Not that he was going to draw attention to it,
because his own face felt hot and his mouth was
tingling where it had touched her skin.

'Let's take five minutes' break,' he said
gruffly, 'because I need to check in with Pascal, and no doubt you want to tell your family where you are.' And five minutes would be
enough to get himself back under strict control.
He'd make sure of it.

After Louisa had spoken to her grandmother
in London and her cousins to let them know
she was staying in Charlmoux until Friday, she
spent a while with Sébastien looking at the constitution and the legal system in the country.

Hortense cooked them a wonderful dish of sole meunière for dinner, which they ate on the patio while they watched the sun set over the sea. They sat sipping a glass of wine as the sky gradually darkened and the stars started to come out.

'So what drives *you*?' Sébastien asked. 'Why do you love fabric so much?'

'I think it's the way it makes me feel,' she said. 'I've always been fascinated by the heritage stuff, so that's why I'm a bit greedy and I work at the Heritage Centre two days a week, and the rest of the time at the studio. It's the best of both worlds, the old and the new.' She smiled. 'Watching Nan make dresses and seeing how people just glowed when they put the dresses on: I wanted to do that for people, too. And I like giving brides and teenagers the dress of their dreams.' She spread her hands. 'I know the dress isn't the most important part of the wedding—marriage itself is the important bit— but a dress makes a difference. Whether it's a wedding or a prom, it's a day when all eyes are going to be on you. It's a lot of pressure, especially if your confidence isn't great to start with. A dress can help you feel confident.'

'Like when you wear your mother's pearls?' he asked.

She nodded. 'Which I now know were my great-grandmother's.'

'I would've stood up for you if Henri had demanded them back,' he said.

'Even if he went Kingzilla on you?'

Sébastien laughed. 'Yes. I'm not scared of him. I respect him—even though I know he's behaved badly where you're concerned—because he's been progressive during his reign and he's trying to make the country as modern as he can. But I think he has a blind spot about his son.'

Louisa sighed. 'He blames my mum for the accident—even though she wasn't there.'

'It's unfair,' Sébastien said, 'though I can understand his thinking. If your dad hadn't married your mum, he wouldn't have been in London that day and the car wouldn't have hit him. Except,' he added, 'your dad might have been in London on business for Charlmoux. But grief makes people act in strange ways.'

'I guess.' She paused. 'Sébastien, thank you for helping me. I'm sorry this is taking up so much of your time.'

'It's not your fault,' he said. 'And it's a pleasure.'

Scarily, it was. She'd seen a different side of him, here—the non-starchy Séb that she thought he might be with his family. And he was starting to let her in. She'd been moved by what he'd told her about his best friend, how he'd felt guilty about not being able to give Marcel enough support; and she'd seen a moment of wistfulness in his face when he'd said how Marcel was settled now. She rather thought that Sébastien was a man who felt deeply, but had taught himself not to show it.

And that changed his suggestion of marriage. Maybe it wouldn't be a business arrangement, after all. Maybe, if she managed to unlock the layers, she'd find a man who'd make her feel the way her mother had felt about her father. The thought was exhilarating and scary at the same time. Could she get to know him properly? Would he let her?

To her surprise, she found herself yawning. 'Sorry. I don't mean to be rude.'

'You're not. It's the sea air making you sleepy,' he said.

'I think I'm going to head for bed,' she said.

'I'll stay out for a bit,' he said. 'The stars are amazing out here, where there's no light from the city to dim them.' Though he stood up politely when she rose from her chair.

On impulse, she walked over towards him, intending to kiss him on the cheek. That sweet kiss on her palm on the way back from the beach had changed things between them, made them easier with each other. But either she'd misjudged or he moved, because she ended up kissing the corner of his mouth instead.

He froze. She was about to apologise and back away when he cupped her face in his hands, and his mouth brushed hers in the softest, sweetest kiss.

'*Bonsoir*, Louisa,' he whispered. 'See you tomorrow.'

She had no idea how she managed to walk into the house and up to her room, because that kiss seemed to have scrambled her brain. And she was still thinking about kissing him when she finally drifted off to sleep.

CHAPTER EIGHT

THURSDAY WAS THEIR last day at the beach house. How had these few days gone by so quickly? Louisa wondered.

'I think we've covered everything major,' Sébastien said at last. 'The only other thing I can think of: did your mum teach you any ballroom dancing as well as ballet?'

'No. Why?' Louisa asked.

'You might have to dance at a charity ball,' he said. 'You should be OK, because you've had some dance training and most of the men will be able to lead you. Or…' He paused. 'I could teach you the basics of the waltz and the foxtrot.'

Her pulse leapt at the idea of dancing with him. 'I'd like that. I've got my turquoise dress with me, and shoes I can dance in.'

'Great. We'll run through it tonight, after dinner.'

It was Hortense's evening off; she'd left them cold poached salmon and salad in the fridge, along with a bowl of strawberries, plus home-made ice cream in the freezer. Sébastien had changed into a suit and Louisa into her turquoise dress. It felt weirdly like a date. Dressed up, dinner and dancing…

Would he kiss her tonight? Or would he remember that tomorrow they were going back to the palace, and keep his distance from her?

As the stars began to shimmer in the darkening sky, Sébastien flicked into a music streaming app on his phone. 'I've found a playlist for the foxtrot. That's a good one to start with.'

The lawn was smooth and flat, feeling like velvet underneath her feet, and it made the perfect dance floor. She concentrated on Sébastien's instructions and learning the steps, though being in his arms was seriously disrupting her ability to think of anything except how it felt to be close to him.

'I think you've got the hang of the foxtrot,' he said. 'Now the waltz.' He flicked into a different song: Louis Armstrong's 'What a Wonderful World'.

"The waltz is easy: just six steps, and you can break them down into two sets of three,' he said. 'What we're going to do is make a kind of box.' He demonstrated. 'Back, side, close, forward, side, close. One-two-three, one-two-three, and you're using alternate legs. Nice and simple.'

He grinned. 'It's way easier than anything you do in a dance fitness class.'

'Maybe.' And maybe she could teach him a few moves from her class. Get hot and sweaty with him…

Oh, help. She needed to concentrate, or instead she'd be standing on his toes.

'Now we need to get into ballroom hold. Put your left hand on my shoulder,' he directed, 'and hold my left hand with your right—we're holding our arms out to give us balance.'

It was a formal hold, but when his right hand was resting on her waist and his left hand was curled with hers, it felt incredibly intimate. If she leaned forward slightly, he'd be in kissing distance. When they started to move to the music, even though all Sébastien was doing was talking her through the steps in the simplest possible terms, Louisa couldn't concentrate. She was too aware of the way their legs were practically sliding between each other's as they moved. This was like making love with their clothes on. And she couldn't shake the idea of making love with Sébastien. Kissing him. Touching him. The final intimacy.

She couldn't think straight, and she couldn't dance straight, either; she stumbled, and he kept her upright. And that made it even worse.

Think of something unsexy, she told herself. Listen to him. Follow the steps.

Except she couldn't think of anything except Sébastien. The warmth of his skin. His clean, masculine scent. How much she wanted to kiss him.

'We're going to turn, though it's not going to be like a ballet pirouette,' he said. 'Just keep going with the steps, and trust me not to steer you wrong.'

Sébastien Moreau was a man of integrity. Over the last week, she'd learned to trust him.

But this was something else. Holding him close, not knowing quite where she was going because she couldn't see behind her—and, when he started turning them, it felt as if she were floating. Swept off her feet. Dancing on air. Every cliché rolled into one, yet making it something new and special and wonderful.

Did he feel it, too?

He'd stopped talking her through the steps, but she didn't need the instructions any more. She was dancing instinctively, following his lead and letting him guide her as they glided round their makeshift dance floor. And how good it felt to be close to him, dancing, together, swooping and swaying and swirling.

At the end of the song, he dropped out of the ballroom hold and cupped her face in his hands.

She opened her eyes and looked at him. His eyes were huge and dark, full of longing.

For her?

She didn't dare ask.

But then she found herself looking at his mouth. The sensual curve of his lower lip. The perfect Cupid's bow of his top lip. And she ached to taste him.

Maybe he could read her feelings in her expression; maybe she'd accidentally said it aloud; or maybe he felt exactly the same way that she did, his body humming with the same need, because he dipped his head and brushed his lips against hers, light as a butterfly's wing. Her mouth tingled where he'd touched her; and it wasn't enough. It wasn't anywhere near enough. She wanted more: she wanted all of him.

'Sébastien,' she whispered, and slid her arms round his neck.

Somehow his hands had moved down to her waist, and he'd drawn her close against him.

All she had to do was rise up on tiptoe and brush her mouth against his, just as tentatively as he'd kissed her. Asking. Offering. Promising.

His arms tightened round her, hers tightened round him, and then they were really kissing. And it felt like the warmth of a spring sun unfurling round her after a long, dark winter. As if she'd finally found where she really belonged.

He broke the kiss. 'Louisa.' His voice was husky, cracked with need. 'The timing's all wrong. We have to go back to the palace tomorrow,' he said.

'But we have tonight,' she said. 'Here and now. Just you and me.'

His eyes darkened and he kissed her again. 'Tell me to stop,' he said, when he'd dragged his mouth from hers.

That was the last thing she intended to do. Instead, she took his hand and pressed a kiss into his palm, the same way that he'd done that first day by the garden gate and put her senses all in a spin. 'I have a question for you. Do you have a condom?'

His breath hitched. 'Louisa, my self-control's hanging by a thread.'

Good. She wanted it to snap. She wanted *him*. All of him. For tonight.

So, instead of being sensible and walking away, she reached up to kiss him.

He kissed her back, his mouth hot and demanding, and she felt as if she were burning up with need and desire.

'Last chance to be sensible,' he said when he dragged his mouth away from hers.

She shook her head. 'I want you, Sébastien. Tonight, you're mine and I'm yours.' They could deal with all the complications tomorrow.

In response, he scooped her up in his arms and carried her into the house. Louisa had never seen him in caveman mode before, and it sent a thrill of desire through her. He kissed her at the foot of the stairs, then carried her up the stairs to his room. He closed the door behind them with his foot, then let her slide down his body until her feet touched the floor again, leaving her in no doubt about just how much he wanted her.

'I've wanted this all week,' he said, his voice husky. 'Maybe even since the first day I met you and you made me feel as if I'd been steam-rollered.'

'That's how you made me feel, too,' she admitted. 'And I want you so badly.'

He kissed her until she was breathless. 'Hold that thought,' he said, and went to close his curtains before switching on his bedside light.

In the dim light, she felt ridiculously shy. Sébastien clearly noticed, because he kissed her lightly. 'If you want to change your mind, Louisa, we can stop now.'

She shook her head. 'I'm not changing my mind. I want you, Sébastien. It's…' She hesitated, unable to find the right words.

'It's scary,' he said. 'There's a risk that doing this might wreck everything.'

'I don't understand why I'm feeling shy with you,' she said.

'It's the getting naked bit,' he said. 'I can turn the light off, if that would help.'

'But then I won't be able to s—' She felt the colour storm into her face as she realised what she was about to confess.

He laughed. 'That goes both ways, Louisa.'

He wanted to see her naked, just as much as she wanted to see him. And the knowledge made her pulse rate leap up a notch.

'I have another idea,' he said. 'You take off a piece of my clothing, and I take off a piece of yours. We'll take it in turns.'

He wanted her to undress him.

To let him undress her.

The idea made her knees go weak and the ends of her fingers started to tingle with adrenalin. 'Except that's not quite fair. You're wearing more than I am,' she pointed out.

He opened his arms. 'Let's not count my jacket and tie. I'm all yours. Do with me what you will,' he invited.

She took his jacket off, then his tie. And then she looked him in the eye as she undid the buttons on his shirt, one by one, the tips of her fingers tingling as they brushed his skin. When she pushed the soft cotton from his shoulders, she caught her breath. He was beautiful. Muscular without being a gym gorilla, with a light sprinkling of hair on his chest, the kind of olive-toned skin that loved the sun, and the most perfect abs.

She wanted to paint him. She wanted to sculpt him. But most of all she wanted to explore every millimetre of him.

'My turn,' he said.

She could feel his hands shaking as he unzipped her dress, stroking down her spine and kissing the nape of her neck. She could see them shaking as she stepped out of her dress and he hung it over the back of a chair; and it made her feel better to know that he was just as nervous about this as she was.

'You're so beautiful,' he said as he turned back to her, the top of his forefinger tracing the lacy edge of her bra. 'I want to touch you, Louisa. Kiss you.' He dragged in a breath. 'All over.'

She wanted it, too. So much that her mouth had gone dry and she couldn't utter a single word. Her fingers just weren't working properly, because she couldn't undo the button of his trousers. The backs of her fingers brushed against the skin of his abdomen, and every nerve end felt as if it was fizzing. In the end, she looked at him. 'Sébastien. I've turned into this incapable mess. And I...' She shook her head. She couldn't even find the right words, now. How pathetic was that?

He kissed her lightly. 'Me, too. I can't think straight when I'm with you.'

'I'm used to sketching dresses—but I want to sketch you. Just like you are now, all rumpled and sexy as hell.' She trailed a finger down his chest; his breath hissed with need and pleasure, sending a thrill through her. She reached up to kiss him again.

Time seemed to stop, and she had no idea which of them had finished undressing the other; all she was aware of was the way Sébastien almost ripped the top sheet off his bed, picked her up and laid her back against the pillows.

They really were going to do this.

Make love.

But she hadn't been prepared for how it felt to be skin to skin with him.

How it felt when his mouth tracked a path down her body, when he licked and nibbled and teased her with the tip of his tongue, making her wriggle impatiently.

How it felt when he touched her, his fingers teasing and caressing, finding out exactly where and how she liked being touched, what made her gasp and hold on to him.

It was as if he was trying to memorise her with his hands and his mouth and his body, the same way she was trying to memorise him. And she wanted to remember every nanosecond of tonight.

Finally he slipped on the condom. 'OK?' he asked.

'Yes,' she said, and he eased into her. He was gentle, giving her time to adjust to him and then he began to move.

This wasn't just satisfying a physical urge, it was a connection deeper than she'd expected; and she really wasn't prepared for how it felt to climax with him buried deep inside her, waves of pleasure that spiralled and bound them closer together. She cried out his name and heard him groan her name in return, shuddering as he reached his own climax. He collapsed next to her, their arms still wound round each other, their breathing rapid.

'I'll be right back,' he whispered, a few moments later. 'But please don't go back to your own room. Stay with me tonight, Louisa. I want to fall asleep with you in my arms. To wake up with you.'

Spend the night with him. Fall asleep in his arms. Wake up and he'd be the first thing she saw.

How could she resist?

'I'll stay,' she said.

She felt as if she was smiling from the inside out when he came back. This felt so right, so

perfect. He slid into bed beside her and drew
the sheet over them before shifting so she was
cuddled into him. He pressed a kiss against the
top of her head, warm and affectionate. And it
felt as if this was the real Sébastien, the one he
kept hidden behind the starchy exterior. He'd let
her close. Trusted her with himself.

Yes, things were a bit complicated in their
lives right now, and she had no idea how this
was going to work out—but she was sure that
they'd find a way. Together.

Sébastien knew when Louisa had finally fallen
asleep; her breathing had slowed and deepened.
Having her curled in his arms, her head pillowed on his shoulder and her arm wrapped
round his waist, was just what he wanted.

He'd known it would be good between them.
But he hadn't guessed how perfect it would be.

Tomorrow, before they went back to the palace, he'd ask her to be his queen again. It was
the practical solution to the problem for both
of them. Sort of. He knew that Louisa wanted
love—the kind of passionate, intense love she'd
seen in the ballet and heard of between her parents; right now, he couldn't offer her exactly
what she wanted. But, with time, he thought
that love would grow between them. They could
have everything: the duty and compatibility

Charlmoux needed, and then over the years the kind of love she wanted.

He just hoped she'd give him a chance.

The next morning, Louisa woke in Sébastien's arms, warm and comfortable. Even though they were going back to the palace today, it was going to be fine—because they'd be together.

Then she realised that Sébastien wasn't asleep. His breathing was shallow and not quite even. Was he simply being kind and letting her sleep in, or had he changed his mind since last night and was lying there, working out how he could back out of this?

Doubts seeped up her spine, turning her cold.

Last night had been perfect. Last night, she'd thought that maybe he felt the same way as she did. That he wanted to be with her for her own sake—that he, too, thought they could find a way through all the political stuff together. But had she been kidding herself? Had she just seen what she'd wanted to see? Was she expecting too much from him? Was he even capable of giving her the love she wanted?

Time to be brave. 'Good morning,' she said.

'Good morning.' His voice was neutral, cool and calm. There was none of the passion she'd seen last night. None of the love. He was obviously back in royal mode.

His next words confirmed it. 'I've been think-ing. These last few days, we've got on really well. We're compatible, in lots of ways. I think our marriage would be a happy one.'

She sagged with disappointment. So he was still seeing it as a business decision, nothing to do with love. Worse still, it sounded as if he as-sumed she was just going to go along with the idea of marrying him.

And she couldn't.

Not when he viewed it as logical, not emo-tional. If she married him for the country's sake, she'd always want something he couldn't give her. In the end, they'd make each other miser-able.

'Compatibility isn't enough, Sébastien,' she said, as gently as she could. 'I want the kind of love my parents had. It's not negotiable.'

Love.

Séb had told himself last night that love would come, in time. But what if it didn't? He'd loved Elodie, but he'd neglected her for his work. He'd neglected his family. What if he neglected Lou-isa, too? What if she ended up resenting him because of that?

And even if she did find this amazing, all-consuming love she seemed to want, what then? She'd still have her duty to the country. Maybe the man of her dreams—he forced himself to ignore the thousand paper cuts of jealousy at the thought that it might not be him—wouldn't be able to cope with the pressure of Louisa's job. And love wouldn't be enough to bolster either of them.

Louisa might want love, but duty would serve her far better. The practical stuff, the stuff she seemed to be ignoring, would protect her far more than love would.

He could tell her he loved her. But her idea of love was something he knew was impractical and fragile—something that would be crushed under the weight of the throne. And what did he know of this all-consuming passion? How could he promise her something he might not be able to give, something he knew he couldn't live up to, even if he tried his best? That wouldn't be fair to either of them.

'I'm sorry, Sébastien. I can't marry you,' she said quietly.

Because she was chasing after rainbows that would vanish and leave her stranded. How could he make her see that what he was offering was something stronger, something that would last? 'Louisa. What you want—it doesn't exist,' he said.

'My parents had it,' she said, her chin tilting at a stubborn angle.

'If your father hadn't died, would it have been enough?'

Her eyes narrowed. 'So you're saying you don't believe my parents loved each other.'

'No. What I'm saying is that love isn't something that stays like that for ever. All the frothy, hearts-and-flowers stuff eventually fades over time. It isn't real. It isn't permanent. It…' He shook his head in frustration. Right now, all he seemed to be doing was pushing her further away. 'You can't ignore the practical stuff. The job's the thing that's all-consuming, not love. You need someone who can cope with that. Someone who will support you properly. Someone who understands the job.' Someone who'd protect her.

'Marriage isn't a job, Sébastien. *Love* isn't a job. And it does exist, even though you're trying to deny it.'

'But feelings change,' he said. 'When the grand passion goes, how do you know that you'll stay together? Once all the sex and the attraction and the excitement has faded, there won't be anything left to support your marriage—or the throne. Whereas if you start with compatibility and understanding, maybe friendship, that's something you can build on.'

'It's not enough,' she said. 'Without love, it's never going to be enough. I can't marry you.'

She'd rejected him. He wasn't enough for her. And he couldn't tell her he loved her. Not the kind of love she was looking for, because it didn't exist. He could offer her loyalty, affection, honour, support—things that would always stay true, and for him added up to a lot more than love—but he couldn't offer her the rainbows she dreamed of.

She dragged in a breath. 'I know it's ridiculous, given last night, but would you mind closing your eyes?'

She was walking out on him?

Well, of course she was. Because he couldn't say what she wanted to hear. And he wouldn't offer her empty promises.

He was an honourable man who always did the right thing, so he did exactly what she'd asked.

He could hear rustling sounds as she dressed. 'I'll see you later. I need to pack,' she said.

When the door closed behind her, he sat up, drawing his legs up and wrapping his arms round his shins, and rested his head on his knees.

He'd taken a gamble.

And lost.

CHAPTER NINE

THE JOURNEY BACK to the palace was hideous. Louisa wore her business suit as if it were armour. When she climbed into the back of the car with Séb, she said, 'You don't mind if I sew, do you?'—and then jammed in her earbuds before waiting for his answer.

He retreated to his laptop, but kept glancing at her in the hope that he could catch her eye and she'd talk to him. But her attention was resolutely fixed on her embroidery.

Back at the palace, she was forced to take out the earbuds.

'The Queen wishes to see you,' he said.

'Of course,' she said, all cool and calm and as starchy as she'd accused him of being.

He'd taught her well. He ought to be proud, instead of feeling as if she'd just eviscerated him.

The footmen took their luggage; he showed her to the drawing room. 'I'll be in my office, if you need anything.'

She looked surprised. 'You're not coming with me?'

'They didn't ask for me,' he said, and gave her his courtliest bow. *À la prochaine.*' Maybe his absence might make her heart grow fonder. Or maybe not.

'You wished to see me, *madame*?' Louisa asked.

Marguerite gave her a hug. 'Welcome back.'

The King was sitting on the sofa. He looked at her and folded his arms. 'It's public knowledge now. You're the heir.'

Louisa mirrored his body language. 'My life is in London. My family, my job, my friends. I can't rule Charlmoux from London, and I don't want to give everything up and move here. Just give me the paperwork to say I renounce all claim, and I'll sign it.'

'You can't,' he said, not looking particularly pleased about it.

'It's true, *ma petite*,' Marguerite said.

Louisa stared at the King. 'Explain to me how you can step down and I can't.'

'The constitution is clear,' Henri said. 'Ill health is the only grounds for standing down from the throne.'

'Can't you just install Sébastien as your regent?'

'No,' Henri said. 'Because you are my granddaughter. You are the heir.'

On the one hand, it was nice to know that he'd come to some kind of acceptance of her. On the other, she was trapped. 'There has to be a way out of this,' Louisa said. 'I don't want to rule. You don't want me to rule. Sébastien has spent years training to take over from you, and he'll do a great job. Can't we tell everyone there's been a mistake and I'm not related to you at all?'

'No,' Marguerite said, 'because that would be tarnishing your father's memory.'

'So I'm stuck,' she said.

'You have family here,' Marguerite said. 'You have a job. You have friends—Sébastien, for a start.'

Louisa willed herself not to blush, thinking about last night. She and Sébastien weren't friends. They'd been lovers, but they weren't friends. Not any more.

'Your father is buried here,' Henri added.

'My mother is buried in London,' she countered.

'The press is full of speculation,' Henri said. 'If you go back to London, they'll follow you. Do you really wish your brides to have to fight their way through your front door? Will your cousins mind being followed down the street with a camera in their faces?'

'That,' she said, 'sounds like blackmail.'

'No. It's how some of the press behave,' he

said. 'Stay for a little longer. Please. We can work out where we go from here. And,' he added, 'your grandmother and Sébastien have shown me the error of my ways.'

She stared at him. 'Meaning?'

'Meaning,' he said, uncrossing his arms, 'that I owe you an apology. I owe your mother an apology.'

The thing she'd wanted and thought he'd never give.

'Louis loved your mother. I should have supported him better. I should have allowed them to marry,' Henri said, 'and I should have let her attend his funeral. But I was angry, and I was grieving. I didn't behave well.' He paused. 'But I want you to be clear that I didn't know about you.'

Would it have made any difference? She wasn't sure. 'You evicted Mum from the flat.'

'I shouldn't have done that, either,' he said.

'She was scared you'd take me from her.'

He flinched. 'I can understand her fears, given how I treated her. I apologise. I...' He blew out a breath. 'I don't know what I would have done. And I can't change the past,' he said. 'But I can learn from it. And I have something to show you.' He patted the seat beside him.

Feeling slightly antsy, she sat down.

He took a folder from the table next to him and handed it to her.

She opened it to discover a plan by a monumental mason, showing a new carving for the slab of Louis' memorial.

*Beloved husband of Catherine
and father of Louisa*

'I—I don't know what to say,' she whispered. There was a huge lump in her throat.

'Sébastien told me what you wanted. I trust this is correct?'

She nodded. 'Thank you.'

'Perhaps,' he said, 'we can have a truce. Start again.'

She smiled. 'I'd like that.'

'*Bien.* Now, I assume you wish to freshen up after your journey.'

It was a dismissal, but a much kinder one than she'd ever expected from him. 'We'll talk later,' she promised.

In return, he patted her hand. Given that he didn't seem the kind of person to give hugs, she knew that was a huge gesture.

'Will you walk with me, *ma petite*?' her grandmother asked.

Louisa nodded, and walked with the Queen through the long gallery.

'Right now,' Marguerite said, 'I would say you're feeling trapped. But I hope that will change, in time. You are the heir, and we can't pretend that you don't exist.'

'I'm not a queen,' Louisa said.

'But you will be, and you'll be a good one.' Marguerite paused. 'Looking back, I think your father felt trapped, too. But, having met you, I think your mother would have supported him so he would have been a good king. You have my support, you have the King's support, and I believe your family in London will support you, too. You can make this work, Louisa.'

'Can I? I'll have to give up so much,' Louisa said. 'I'll hardly see my family. I'll have to leave London. And I love my job.'

'It's about finding a workable compromise,' the Queen said. 'Your family will always be welcome here, and video calls will help in between. You can still visit London. And you don't have to give up all of the textile work you love— you can make time in your schedule for yourself. The pleasure will be all the sweeter when time is so precious.'

Something about the Queen's tone and those last few words made Louisa wonder. 'Just how ill is the King?'

'Sicker than he will admit,' Marguerite said.

'But if you need him to stay on for another year, until you're ready, then he'll do it.'

'He needs to step down,' Louisa said, 'and you all need me to step up.'

'Talk to Veronica,' Marguerite said. 'You can perhaps say things to her that you wouldn't feel comfortable saying to me. Talk to Sébastien.'

Ironic: the Queen expected her to open up to a man who wouldn't open up to her. Though she did need to see Sébastien, to thank him for persuading her grandfather to change the wording on her father's grave.

'Take your time,' Marguerite said, squeezing her hand. 'And I'm here if you need me.'

'Thank you,' Louisa said, and went to find Sébastien. She got slightly lost on the way to his office, but a footman stepped in to help.

He looked up from his desk when she knocked on the door. 'Was there something you needed?'

'To thank you,' she said. 'The King showed me the monumental mason's plan for the new wording.'

He shrugged. 'It was the right thing.'

Which was what drove him, she knew. 'How did you persuade him?'

'We talked,' Sébastien said—as always, giving none of his feelings away.

'I…um—' She glanced at Pascal.

'You can say anything in front of Pascal. He's discreet,' Sébastien said.

'The King says I can't step down. That the only reason for stepping down is ill health.'

'I did warn you,' he said quietly.

Sébastien had also offered her a way out. But she'd already turned him down, so it was no longer an option. 'I'm staying for a bit longer,' she said. 'Until we work out where we go from here.'

'I'd say that would be a press conference, shadowing the King for a while, and then a coronation after the King steps down at the end of the summer—or maybe he'll delay it until you're ready,' he said.

'What about you?'

He shrugged. 'I'll resign at a suitable point.'

Resign? Leave the palace? But this was everything he'd worked for. He was losing just as much as she was. Changing his life because of her. 'That's—'

'It is what it is,' he cut in. 'Was there anything else?'

It wasn't a discussion she wanted to have with him in front of anyone else, but it was pretty clear Sébastien had no intention of being alone with her. 'No. It's fine. But thank you.'

De rien.

And he was in full starch mode, because his smile didn't reach his eyes.

Right now, he was more distant than she'd ever known him; and he clearly wanted her to go. 'I, um… I'll catch you later.'

She spent the next hour talking things through with her grandparents in London. Another hour walking in the palace gardens and thinking about it. Another hour sewing, concentrating on the stitches while she worked things through in the back of her head.

And then she went to see the King and Queen.

'I've talked to Nan and Granddad,' she said. 'And I've thought about it. If my dad had still been alive, he would've been the heir and I would've followed in his footsteps. I chose to join my family's firm in London; and now it's time I chose to join the family firm here.'

'You're sure about this, *ma petite*?' the Queen asked.

Louisa nodded. 'You said about finding a workable compromise. That's what we'll do. And we'll make it the best for everyone.'

Sébastien had taught her that.

He'd also taught her that she had to choose between love and duty. She still didn't agree. But until he was prepared to see there was an alternative, there was nothing she could do but wait.

* * *

'You look—' Pascal began.

Séb shook his head. 'Don't even go there, please.'

'She doesn't really want to do the job. You do. There has to be a way round it.'

There was. But Louisa had rejected it. Rejected *him*. And Emil had tipped him off that Louisa had agreed to step up and be the heir. Between them, perhaps he and Emil could advise Louisa to appoint Pascal as her private secretary; he'd do an excellent job of supporting her.

But her life wouldn't include Sébastien himself.

'No,' Séb said.

He didn't eat with her, that evening; as far as he knew, she ate with the King and Queen.

He spent the weekend catching up with paperwork; hers was spent in a press conference, as he'd predicted. He watched it at his desk, and she completely charmed her audience. The preparation he'd coached her through had paid off. Which was a good thing, he reminded himself. He wanted her to do well. To be reconciled with her grandparents. For the country to be stable.

Just…he wished it had been different. That he'd been by her side.

Despite the fact that she lived in the apartment opposite his, he managed to avoid her for the next couple of days. But he missed her. He missed her with a visceral ache he hadn't expected. Walking in the garden made him miserable, because he remembered walking there with her; and it brought back memories of the way they'd danced together in the gardens of the beach house. How they'd waltzed. How they'd kissed. How they'd ended up making love.

He'd intended to teach her how to be a princess, but somewhere along the way he'd fallen in love with her.

And he really didn't know what to do about it.

She wanted love. He knew that. But had he left it too late to offer her love? Would she believe him, if he told her how he felt? Or would she think he was just trying to talk her into a marriage for the country's sake?

After another poor night's sleep, he was pacing the palace gardens when he rounded a corner and almost bumped into her.

'Sorry,' he said.

'No harm done,' she replied. Then her eyes narrowed. 'Are you all right?'

He lifted his chin. 'Yes, of course.' And then he sighed. Maybe he should tell her the truth. 'No. I'm as miserable as hell.'

'Why?'

'Because,' he said, 'something happened when we were at the beach house.'

Colour stormed her cheeks.

He shook his head. 'Not that,' he said. 'Though that, as well.'

'I'm not following.'

'According to Pascal, I'm not making a lot of sense to anyone, nowadays,' he said dryly. 'Can we talk?'

She nodded, and he walked with her towards the wildflower meadow.

'Something I never told you: when I agreed to be the heir, I was dating someone seriously,' he said. 'Her name was Elodie. We'd been law students together. I loved her, and I hoped we had a future together. But she really, really hated life at the palace. The press were always in her face. It got in the way of her work. And she didn't see enough of me, because I was too busy trying to learn everything I needed for my new role and I neglected her. In the end, she told me she couldn't do it any more. She didn't actually give me the ultimatum, but the choice was obvious: love or duty. I chose duty. And maybe I made the wrong choice.'

Louisa wasn't sure what surprised her more: that Sébastien had been serious about someone, or that he was admitting to being wrong. But what had happened with Elodie explained why he didn't believe in love, and why he'd insisted that love had no place in a royal marriage. In his experience, love had been versus duty rather than supporting it.

'Do you still love her?' Because, if he did, he should never have made love with Louisa.

'No. In any case, she's happily married, and she has two children and a flourishing career as a family lawyer—the life she wanted and the life she deserves. I don't mean...' He sighed. 'Why is this so difficult to explain?'

Probably because he was talking about his feelings. But if he was actually going to open up to her, she didn't want him to stop. 'Keep talking. It doesn't matter if it's muddled. Just talk,' she said.

He nodded. 'When I say the wrong choice, I mean I was wrong about love. I thought I could manage without it. And I've discovered that I can't.' He stopped at the edge of the flower meadow. 'Shall we sit?'

'Sure.' She sat down opposite him.

'The last few days have been unbearable,' he said.

'Because you're no longer the heir?'

'It's not that,' he said. 'It's you. You were just the other side of the corridor, but you might as well have been at the edge of the universe.' He paused. 'I discovered that I miss you. And duty isn't enough, any more. I want...'

She held her breath.

'I want you,' he said finally, and looked her in the eye.

His feelings blazed from his eyes: but she needed to hear him say it. Needed him to open up to her. So she simply waited for him to go on.

'I didn't expect,' he said, 'to fall in love with you.' He broke off a few stems of flowers, and began to weave them together. 'And it was everything about you. In London, when you told me off in the café. When you showed me the magic of ballet and made me realise how your father had seen your mother. Here, when you brought the sunshine back into the Queen's face and you were kind to the King, even though you were justifiably angry with him. When you cooked with me, and it felt like being a family.'

Just how it had felt for her.

'At the beach house, when you were determined to learn and make things work. On the beach, when you held my hand. And that last night, when we waltzed together under the stars... I wanted to fall asleep in your arms. I wanted you to be the first thing I saw when I woke. Except the wrong words came out.' He blew out a breath. 'I want to marry you. But it's got nothing to do with us being compatible and being able to rule the country together, and everything to do with the fact that I love you and I can't function without you. Without you, it's like a bit of me's missing. The better part of me.'

Sébastien loved her.

He really loved her.

'And this is all too little, and too late, and too hopeless. I know that. You're going to be busy, just as I was. You don't have time for any of this. I'll do the right thing: I'll resign from my office at the palace and disappear quietly,' he said. 'But I didn't want to go without telling you how I feel about you. And telling you to your face that you're right. Without love, marriage is worth nothing.'

'So what do you want, Sébastien?'

'Really?'

'Really.'

'I want you,' he said. 'And I don't mean *la Princesse* Louisa. I mean I want Louisa Gallet. I'd like to start again. Ask you to date me. Walk through the lavender fields with me at sunset. Watch the sun rise over the sea. Maybe come to the farm and help with the harvest, even if you can only spare a couple of hours.'

'Is that what you're going to do? Go back to the farm?' she asked.

'For a bit,' he said. 'While I work out what to

do next. If I want to practise law, I'll need more training.'

'What about all the work you've done here?'

'It's not the right sort of work for me to be a barrister or solicitor,' he said. 'But in the meantime I can make myself useful to my family.'

'Duty,' she said.

He shook his head. 'Love. I love my family. I've neglected them, too.' He blew out a breath. 'So now I've told you the truth. I neglected the woman I intended to marry, and I neglected my family. I was worried I would neglect you, too, and you'd end up resenting me.'

'Or maybe,' she said, 'you just need to learn that love and duty can work together. I've talked to my grandparents about compromise.'

'Is that why you're staying?'

'Even the brightest lawyer I know can't get me out of taking over from my grandfather,' she said. 'I worked for my mum's family firm in London. Now it's time to work for my dad's family firm.'

He looked down at the flowers he'd plaited into a crown. 'As the Queen.'

'From the end of the summer,' she said. 'Though I could do with a consort.' She tipped her head to one side. 'If you know anyone who might be interested in the job?'

'That depends,' he said. 'Because I've learned

something over the last few days. I've learned that, without love, nothing is enough.' He looked at her. 'So where do we go from here? Do you think you could learn to love me?'

He'd been honest with her. It was her turn to be honest with him. 'I already do,' she said. 'I think I did right from the start. Even when I thought we were on opposite sides, you made me tingle. And here in Charlmoux you always made me feel you were on my side, supporting me instead of taking over.'

'Good, because that's what I was trying to do.'

'And you made things happen—things I couldn't do for myself. You got my grandfather to apologise and change the wording on my father's memorial. You introduced me to my grandmother.'

'And I screwed up,' he reminded her. 'I hurt you, and I'm so sorry.'

'We all screw up,' she said. 'As my grandfather told me, you can't change the past, but you can learn from it. And you're bright enough to be a quick learner.'

'Right now,' he said, 'I think you have more confidence in me than I do.'

'I do,' she said, 'because you're a good man. You have integrity. You try to do the right thing, and you want to make the world a better place. But that isn't why I love you.'

'Why do you love me?' he asked.

'That's the thing,' she said. 'Some things you can't explain. You just feel. Like when you watch someone dance *Swan Lake*. You can dissect the techniques, the choreography, the costumes—but none of that can explain how it makes you *feel*. You don't need to explain feelings. They don't have to be neat and tidy and packaged away. They just *are*.'

'And you make me feel, Louisa. You really do.' He paused. 'I thought I had to choose between love and duty. You showed me that I'd got it completely wrong.'

'So now you want it all?'

'I want you,' he said. 'Which is the same thing. So will you consider dating me?'

He wanted to date her.

He'd asked her for herself, not for the crown.

Finally, finally, he was opening up to her. 'What if,' she said, 'I want more than that?'

'If I could, I'd give you the sun, the moon and the stars,' he said.

'That isn't what I want,' she said. 'I want something a lot more precious than that. A lot bigger than that.' She met his gaze. 'I want your heart, Sébastien Moreau.'

'You have my heart,' he said. 'And my love.'

He shifted so he was on one knee. 'And you want more than dating? So do I. Louisa Gallet, you make me want to be a better man, and I'll love you to the end of our days. I haven't got a ring to offer you—but I'd want you to choose it with me anyway, because you're my partner and I'll always listen to what you want. Will you marry me, Louisa? Not for duty, not for convenience, but for love?'

'Did you ask the King's permission to propose to me?' she asked.

'No, because your hand isn't his to give. It's *yours*.'

'Yes,' she said.

'Yes, it's your choice, or yes, you'll marry me?' he asked.

'Both.'

She saw the moment realisation hit, and it was as if the sun lit him up from the inside.

'I love you,' he said softly, and he kissed her.

Then he picked up the crown he'd plaited. Marguerites and cornflowers.'

'My grandmother's name, and my mother's yes,' she said.

He placed the crown on her head. 'These flowers will fade, but you'll always be my princess. My queen.'

'And you,' she said, 'will always be my Sébastien.' She kissed him, and stood up. 'Come on. We have news to share.'

He got to his feet and took her hand. 'One day I'll buy you a proper tiara.'

'I don't need diamonds. I'm keeping this one,' she said. 'I'll press it. And one day we'll show our children how their father proposed to me— with a crown of cornflowers and marguerites.'

EPILOGUE

Two years later

VERONICA MADE A last adjustment to Louisa's veil. 'You look beautiful,' she said. 'Every inch a queen, wearing your mum's pearls.'

'I look like a queen because I have the very best dressmaker,' Louisa said. 'The one my mum would've chosen, if she'd been getting married in the cathedral.' The same cathedral where Louisa had been crowned Queen of Charlmoux two summers ago.

'Your mum and dad would've been so proud of you,' Veronica said, her voice thick with emotion. 'I love you.'

'Love you, too,' Louisa said. 'And I'm so glad we have video calls, so at least I get to see you whenever I want, even if Granddad has to give you the hugs for me.'

'Last check,' Sam said. 'Something old?'

'Mum's pearls,' Louisa said.

'New?' Milly asked.

'Dress.'

'Borrowed?' Nina, Louisa's best friend and the third bridesmaid, asked.

'Mémére's tiara.' The one Marguerite had worn on her own wedding day. Louisa looked at her other grandmother and smiled.

'And blue's your bouquet,' Veronica finished.

Louisa had chosen white roses, like the ones in her mother's bouquet, combined with the cornflowers and marguerites that Sébastien had made into a crown for her, the day he'd asked her to marry him for love.

'Check: fairy flower girls?' Sam asked.

'*Oui!*' Sébastien's nieces chorused, beaming their heads off and making their fairy wings— made for them personally by Louisa—shimmer.

'Your grandfathers are waiting downstairs,' Veronica said. 'Time to go.'

Between them, the bridesmaids managed the train of Louisa's dress down the sweeping staircase. The dress was a simple silk sheath with a three-metre detachable train, overlaid with lace that matched the foliage curls of her tiara and formed the high neck and sleeves.

Jack and Henri were waiting for them at the bottom of the stairs.

'It's how I thought your mum would look,' Jack said, his voice hoarse.

'My Louis would be proud of you,' Henri added, not to be outdone. *'Ma petite-fille.'*

Sam and Milly helped her into the golden carriage drawn by four white horses, while Nina shepherded the flower girls to one of the limos and Jack and Henri climbed into the other side of the carriage. Then the grandmothers of the bride and the bridesmaids climbed into the other limo to follow the carriage to the cathedral.

'Wave out of the window,' Henri said to Jack. 'You're her grandfather, too, and they want to see you.'

Louisa hid a smile and waved out of the carriage windows at the people lining the streets. People were waving madly, cheering and clapping as the carriage went past; there were banners bearing her initial with Sébastien's in hearts.

When they arrived at the cathedral, there was a barrage of media photographers waiting for her. Although all she wanted to do was to walk down the aisle to Sébastien, she also knew the people of Charlmoux wanted to share these moments, so she posed patiently.

Finally her grandmothers went into the cathedral; Nina checked her train, and then Louisa tucked a hand into the crook of each grandfather's arm and the usher held the door for them to enter.

As they walked down the carpet, the pianist and cellist started playing Einaudi's 'Le Onde', which always reminded her of walking on the beach hand in hand with Sébastien at the edge of the sea; the sun was streaming through the clerestory windows, and the whole thing felt magical.

He was waiting for her at the altar, and her heart skipped a beat.

He turned to look at her and smiled, and she knew that everything was going to be just fine.

Jack stopped and lifted her veil. 'I love you. Be happy,' he whispered.

'I love you, too,' Henri added. 'Be happy.'

Louisa smiled, and stepped forward to join Sébastien at the altar.

The archbishop welcomed them, and delivered a sermon all about love. Sébastien held her hand as Jack read Shakespeare's *Sonnet 116*, and then Henri read an excerpt from Thomas à Kempis's *De Imitatio Christi*.

They said their vows, exchanged rings, and finally the archbishop declared them husband and wife, saying, 'You may now kiss the bride.'

Sébastien smiled, mouthed, 'I love you,' and leaned in to kiss her.

After they'd signed the register and a last blessing from the archbishop, they walked down the aisle together and posed for the press on the cathedral steps. To the cheers of the crowd, Sébastien kissed his bride. The rest of the wedding guests lined up on either side, then threw dried cornflower and marguerite petals as confetti while Sébastien and Louisa walked down to the waiting carriage.

On the short journey back to the palace, Louisa and Sébastien held hands and waved with their free hands.

'Well, now, *la Reine* Louisa of Charlmoux,' Sébastien said at the reception, after the food and speeches. 'Are you ready for our first dance?'

'Our first married dance, *le Prince* Sébastien.' Her grandfather, before stepping down, had made his granddaughter's future consort an official prince. She smiled. 'Now the train's detached from my dress, yes. I don't think I could have danced with the train.'

'You look amazing. You *are* amazing,' he said.

When they walked onto the dance floor, the band started playing 'What a Wonderful World'—the song he'd first taught her to waltz to.

'It doesn't get any better than this,' Sébastien said.

'Oh, but it does.' Louisa smiled. 'I have some very hot-off-the-press news for you.'

'What?'

'I seem to have followed in my mother's footsteps. Falling in love with a prince of Charlmoux, and…'

His eyes widened. 'Are you telling me…?'

She whispered in his ear, 'Yup. I discovered this morning, in seven and a half months' time, you'll be meeting someone who's the second in line to the throne of Charlmoux. It's why I had my very own bottle of champagne—or, as our waiter is sworn to keep secret, sparkling elderflower.' Then she pulled back slightly, so she could see his reaction.

In answer, he gave her the widest, widest smile, picked her up and spun her round. 'I love you,' he said. 'Both of you. My queen, and our prince or princess baby…'

* * * * *

If you enjoyed this story, check out these other great reads from Kate Hardy

One Week in Venice with the CEO
Snowbound with the Brooding Billionaire
Surprise Heir for the Princess
Soldier Prince's Secret Baby Gift

All available now!